Hey.

♡ Amy

STILL
BEAUTIFUL

Book Four of the 20 SOMETHING series

Amy Patrick

Cover design by Gabrielle Prendergast at Cover Your Dreams
Formatting by Polgarus Studio

CONTENTS

CHAPTER ONE
GUESS WHO

So I'm the smart one. That's what my parents have said—well, *Momma* has said—since I was a little kid. I have a sister three years older and about twenty-five times prettier than me. And that's fine. I don't resent her—it's not her fault. Besides, who wouldn't want to be intelligent? Smart's cool, right? There's only one problem. For a smart girl, I sure can be stupid.

It's ninety degrees, at least a hundred-fifty-percent humidity, and I'm standing on top of a TV news satellite truck. Not the most comfortable spot I could've picked on a late May afternoon in Georgia. But it's my job—well, kind of—it's my paid internship.

"Okay, Cinda—you see the hydraulic antenna controller?"

"It's kind of hard to miss. Which valve is stuck?" Wiping sweat from my eyes, I peer down over the edge of the high-profile vehicle at the reddening bald head of Frank, the chief engineer at WATV, Atlanta's *Number One News Source,* according to their latest promo campaign.

For the remaining two weeks of my internship he's my boss, and I may not live through it. The reason *I'm* on top of the sat truck is he's too... um... how do I say this nicely? The cumulative effects of his lifelong eating habits prevent him from safely climbing and balancing atop slippery raised surfaces. Seriously— the man's pushing four hundred. And he's got to be at least sixty. When I saw him starting up the ladder, I volunteered for truck-top duty.

"Okay—I think I found it. What should I do? Turn the valve?" I reach toward the sticky valve socket with the wrench Frank provided.

"Wait! Make sure you're not under the dish when you turn it." His frantic warning stops me cold. "It could fall on you. Those things are heavy."

No kidding. "Thanks," I yell back and move to a slightly safer spot on the truck roof before attempting the maneuver again.

This is all new for me. I've already done co-ops at Georgia Power and Light and Coca Cola for my double-engineering major at Georgia Tech. That covered the industrial and systems engineering end. Mechanical engineering is a totally different animal. After spending the first semester of my junior year interning with an automobile manufacturer, I thought it would be fun to finish out the year working in TV, like my sister Kenley. She's a producer for WNN, Worldwide News Network, and loves it. Unfortunately, they only offer unpaid internships, and God knows I need the money, so I took the position here instead.

Of course, money doesn't do you any good if you're squashed like road kill on I-75 at rush hour. I send up a little prayer, brace myself, and turn the valve. The enormous dish drops a few inches, but thankfully, no more than that.

"Got it. It's loose."

"Great. Good job. Okay, let me get inside the truck and see if the electronic controls will move it now. Stay up there, okay?" Frank says.

I slide to a sitting position on the hot surface and mutter, "Sure. Nowhere I'd rather be."

I've been Frank's number one favorite person since he figured out I was capable of working on most of the equipment around here. The man's counting days until his retirement, and he'd probably just sit back and let me do everything if he thought he could get away with it. That's fine with me—I like to be busy, and the more I learn in my five month stint here, the better prepared I'll be for a career after graduation.

The dish moves, I'm still alive, and another day of work is almost in the books. I slide my ID card, step through the back door of the station, and go to the ladies' room to try to clean up a bit—my hands are covered in some sort of greasy black goop which the cheap bulk-marketed hand soap is barely touching. Ten minutes and ten paper towels later, I head back for the engineering department, passing through the enormous WATV newsroom to get there.

"Hey—you—intern. What's your name again?" A chirpy little brunette in retro black glasses motions to me from the assignment desk.

I've met her at least three times. "It's Cinda." What could she want with me? I cross over to her and try to see over the high counter of the assignment desk—it's almost like a crow's nest overlooking a sea of partition-divided desks in the busy newsroom. The girl, whose name *I* remember, Alissa, has disappeared from view. And then she's back. Her owlish-cute face pops over the top of the desk, and she hands down a piece of printer paper.

"Okay, so we're sending you out with Blake. Y'all are going over to the Tech campus—I figured you'd be able to help him find the right building and a good parking spot—I hear it's a nightmare over there."

She must think I'm a news intern—*I've been here four months, for Pete's sake.* I stand on tiptoe to speak to her, but she's disappeared again. I raise my voice, trying to be heard. "Yes, it is but—I'm not—"

My protest is interrupted by a barrage of disconcerting sensations. A huge pair of hands covers my eyes, a warm (and very hard) male chest presses against my back, and I'm surrounded by possibly the best scent I've ever experienced—a mixture of cologne and warm skin and a fruity scent—gum maybe?

Against my ear, a low murmur sends chills spreading across my body like water rippling across a pond. "Guess who?"

The voice is deep and raspy, a Southern-tinged baritone… and it's completely unfamiliar.

The close proximity of the assignment desk prevents me from stepping forward out of his grasp, so I jerk to the side and out of the arms of the delicious-smelling stranger who has obviously mistaken me for someone else. I whirl around to face him and get a quick, dazzling impression of green eyes and strong features, and barely controlled waves of auburn hair.

The green eyes go wide, and then his color deepens—wow—*that was a fast blush response.* And wow *WOW*—this guy is super-hot. He reminds me of the actor from that Scottish highlander time travel show I've been obsessed with lately. I've been spending *way* too much time alone with cable TV.

"Oh. Uh—sorry. I thought you were… someone else. I'm so sorry." His blush deepens even further.

My God, he is cute. He's probably about Kenley's age—twenty-three—but he looks like a little boy in this moment, stammering and reaching toward me in a placating gesture, then apparently thinking better of it and pulling his hands back to himself. Really nice hands, too, big and strong-looking with those raised veins that guys who work out always seem to have.

Dragging my eyes from his hands to his face, I shake my head. "It's okay. No problem." I offer my own hand to show there are no hard feelings. "I'm Cinda. I'm an intern—not news—engineering."

The guy seems to recover himself. He takes my hand and gives me a smile. *Wow wow wow.* Dimples. The high kind that are almost on the cheekbone. I love those. And *lord help me* he has a dimple in his chin as well.

"I'm Blake," he says. "Not engineering. News. I'm a reporter—just started this week."

"Oh—" I look down at the paper in my other hand. It's some sort of itinerary. "I think this is for you. Alissa at the assignment desk gave it to me—it has something to do with a story at Georgia Tech?"

"Yeah—I was just coming to see her about it."

"I think she's confused. I *do* go to Georgia Tech, but I'm not here to go out with the reporters," *Oh God.* Talk about your Freudian slips. "I mean—out on *stories* with the reporters. I'm just passing through the newsroom, heading back to engineering. To see Frank. My boss."

"You sure?" Blake smiles at me again. "No mercy for the new guy? I could use some expert navigational advice. I hear that campus is like a maze." He tilts his head to the side and raises his brows in a pleading expression.

I laugh at his attempt to appear helpless. "You're a big boy. I'm sure you can manage it alone."

"I'm not sure I want to." His tone is playful and flirty, and those dimples are doing their best to persuade me.

An unfamiliar spark of excitement riffles through the center of my body, leaving a chill in its wake. I take an extra breath. "I…

have to get back to work. And you have to go. Doesn't that say five o'clock?" I gesture to the paper in his hand.

Without looking down he answers. "It does." Then he does look down—at his feet—and back up at me. "You're not a freshman are you?" He does this funny little wince-grin, waiting for my answer.

Now it's my turn to blush. I know I look young. I don't wear makeup, and I'm usually dressed like I'm ready for a pickup game of soccer or lacrosse. I shake my head. "No. I'll be a senior in the fall."

"So that makes you…" He squints his eyes, studying me, trying to guess my age.

"Twenty," I say.

His grin spreads like the sun setting over the ocean at Tybee Island. "Twenty. Okay, Miss-Cinda-who's-twenty. You'll be here tomorrow?"

"Yes," I say, smiling, stepping back away from him as he turns to leave the newsroom and wondering why he cares.

He stops and turns back. "Sorry if I spooked you earlier. I can't believe how much you look like my friend."

"Is that… a good thing or a bad thing?"

He shakes his head, smiling over a good memory. "A very good thing. She was the prettiest girl I'd ever met." He pauses then adds with a dip of his chin and another flash of those incredible dimples, "*Was.*"

Then he spins and leaves the newsroom, and I draw on every sensible fiber of my being, trying not to melt into an uncharacteristic puddle of bliss right there in front of the assignment desk.

CHAPTER TWO
A GOOD MATCH

Great. I'm totally sunburned. I'm studying my crispy red face in the mirror of our apartment's guest bathroom when Kenley comes in from work.

She steps into the powder room doorway, and her face contorts in horror. "Oh Cinda. Your skin. Did they have you working on the surface of the sun today?"

"Close—I was up on top of a live truck—lots of hard reflective surfaces. How was your show?"

"Fantastic. Larson's mom agreed to do an interview with us. I'm completely guilty of nepotism, and I don't even care." She giggles.

Kenley was recently promoted to associate producer of Inside Style, a fashion and lifestyle news program on WNN's evening lineup. Her promotion enabled the two of us to rent this apartment together and finally get out from under the thumb of our meddling and severely priority-confused mother.

Of course, I won't be able to keep her as a roommate much longer. She got engaged a few months ago to Larson Overstreet, the host of WNN's Overstreet Live, and the son of famous fashion designer Corina Videau.

I'm happy for her, but selfishly worried for *me*. I'll never be able to afford this apartment on my own, and I'd rather live on the streets of downtown Atlanta than move back in with my parents.

"If you're not going to wear makeup, you should at least start wearing some sunblock. That must hurt like a bee-sting," Kenley says.

"It's not so bad," I lie. "Anyway, my face needed some color."

"Well, you got that and then some. You *know* anytime you want to learn, I'd be thrilled to teach you to do makeup."

I roll my gaze over to her and grin, painfully. "Yes, I've known that since I was five and you were eight and started painting me up like Dolly Parton. If I ever decide to cross over to the dark-and-glam side, you'll be the first to know."

I poke one cheek and watch as the bright white circle gradually fades and blends back in with my skin's overall tomato-esque tone. Maybe I *should* let her put some makeup on me—just for tonight?

I have a date with a guy from my Heat Transfer class, and—never mind—he's not likely to care. And I don't really *care* if he cares.

"So, where you going with—what's his name?" Kenley asks.

"Troy. A movie, I guess. He picked it out, won't tell me which one. Says it's a *surprise*." I roll my eyes.

"Oooh. That sounds fun. I love it when guys plan things out and make it special."

"I doubt that's it. He was probably just stalling because he doesn't know what's playing. His course load is as heavy as mine, and he's interning with Georgia Power this semester."

Troy is fine. He's a nice guy and really smart, but not exactly full of surprises. We have similar interests—mainly school-related. I like him. But he doesn't *do* anything for me. Not that anyone really does. What Kenley and Larson have is the exception rather than the rule. I don't expect it to happen for me.

A flash of red hair and dazzling dimples fills my vision before I blink it away. I lean closer to the mirror and frown at my reflection. Wow—maybe I got heatstroke as well as sunburn today.

"Well, it sounds to me like *both* of you need to lighten up and get a life," Kenley gently chides. "Have fun tonight. I'll be over at Larson's so don't wait up for me."

I laugh. "Never do. I think only your wardrobe actually lives here now, and you only come by to visit it."

"That is not true. I like to see you, too." She gives me a guilty grin. "Please don't tell Momma and Daddy, okay? I really don't want to hear it."

"You know I never tell her anything. Are you bringing Larson to their house tomorrow night?"

"Yep. So you don't have to worry about what you wear. Momma won't notice *either* of us—she'll be too busy kissing up to her future son-in-law-slash-meal-ticket."

"Poor Larson."

An unspoken understanding passes between us as our eyes meet in the mirror. Thank God for Kenley. No one else in the world would believe, much less understand, the family we grew up in. At least we have each other to complain to.

#

She drops me off to meet Troy at the theater. He wanted to pick me up at my apartment, but I said no. It didn't make any sense. His apartment is right next to the theater, so why should he drive over to my place and then turn around and drive right back there?

I spot him standing near the bank of doors at the theater's entrance. As I get closer, I realize he's sort of dressed up—well, the college-guy version of dressed up. He's got on khakis and a collared shirt. And he's holding something. A flower. Oh no. So it's a *date* date then. I look down at my shorts and Tech t-shirt. Well, too late now.

His face breaks into a smile. "Hi Cinda. How was your day? How were things at the TV station?"

I return his smile. "Good. It was fine. I worked outside a lot of the day. Sorry I didn't get a chance to change." I blanch at my own less-than-truthful statement, but then forgive myself. It sounds nicer than the truth—*I didn't really care enough to dress up for you.*

"No. You're fine. You always look great." He gives me the flower and leans in for a hug, making me also wish I'd taken the time to wash my hair when I showered after work. *What is wrong with me?* I clearly missed out on the girly-girl gene—Kenley got the whole portion of that DNA allotment to our family. I stiffly hug Troy back and we walk inside together.

"I know we usually split it, but I went ahead and got the tickets already—hope you don't mind. I thought we could see *Love You More?* It's a romantic comedy."

"Sure. That's great." I'd probably rather see the Marvel space hero adventure that's showing, but then looking at the life-sized standup display of its main star, a redhead with green eyes and a rogue-ish grin, I decide *maybe not.* I don't need anything else to lure my mind back to where it's been returning all day—that brief encounter with Blake and his maddeningly good smell, his big hands, his smile.

"What did you say?" I ask Troy, realizing he's been talking and I haven't exactly been listening.

"I said I hope it's good. I heard it's really sweet."

"I'm sure it is." I smile at him as we enter the dim theater. He really is a nice guy. A total beta, which is just what I'm looking for. Someone like my dad, who has that same easygoing, calm, undemanding demeanor I find so relaxing. As much as I work *not* to be like my mom, I recognize her intensity in myself. I can't help it. So it makes sense to seek out a beta personality. Troy and I are a good match.

He lets me choose our seats—middle-middle (halfway up, halfway in)—and the theater goes fully dark. About twenty minutes into the movie, which goes way past sweet into sappy, Troy's hand closes around mine on the armrest. Though I feel nothing, save for the additional warmth of his skin and the scratch of a callous on his palm, I don't pull away. This is good. This is our third date, and it's probably about time for some physical contact of some sort.

The couple on the big screen embraces and dives into a very enthusiastic first kiss. Troy's hand squeezes mine a bit tighter. I glance over at him. Maybe *we* should kiss. Yes, probably. I should plan on that. If he doesn't initiate it tonight then I will.

The thought doesn't scare me. It doesn't give me any anticipatory tingles either. I don't really get that *ever*. I sort of suspect my friends who go on and on about sex are joking, exaggerating, or practicing wishful thinking.

I *might* have felt the beginning of tingles once—with my high school boyfriend Tyler. He was three years older, blonde and beautiful, a great kisser—and as it turned out, completely in love with Kenley instead of me. She didn't go out with him, of course. But that didn't make it suck any less when he admitted he'd been dating me just to get close to her. A confession that came *after* I gave him my virginity.

I redirect my attention to the movie. *Good God* it's mushy. What kind of guy even says that stuff in real life? No one—that's who.

"I've never felt this way about anyone before," the onscreen hero says to his lady love.

I snort.

Troy looks over at me, clearly startled out of his immersion in the scene.

"Sorry," I whisper. I couldn't help it. It was just so ridiculous. We should have gone to the space adventure movie.

As we file out of the theater amid the smiling crowd, Troy reaches for my hand and gives me an apologetic look. "So—sorry if that wasn't a good choice."

"No. It was fine. It was cute," I lie. "Did you like it?"

"*I* did. But you didn't seem to really get into it."

"Well, actually, I'm not really that big on rom-coms," I admit. "Maybe we can go to one of those rock climbing places next time or something. Or go to a Braves game."

Troy's worried expression lifts at my apparent willingness to go out again. "Yeah. That sounds great."

We go to dinner at a nearby restaurant famous for its chicken tenders, where I pick up the tab to keep things even. We chat comfortably about subjects where we do have common ground— the important stuff—school and our internships.

"Are you liking Georgia Power?" I ask. Troy is a year ahead of me, a senior, but I actually interned at the company before him, the summer after my freshman year. Last summer I worked for Coca Cola. Georgia Tech has partnerships with all these big companies so their students can not only get hands-on experience, but also class credit and make some money as well.

I'm a little worried about my inability to land a paying internship for this summer. I'm running out of time, and all I've found so far are plenty of companies willing to have me, but none willing to pay. If I don't find one soon, I'll have to line up some other kind of job, and that could be tough with my summer class load.

"It's challenging but it's great. I've made some good connections. I'm hoping it might lead to something permanent there," Troy says.

"I wouldn't doubt it," I assure him.

Troy's one of the top students in his class, so this internship could certainly lead to a post-grad job for him. One of the reasons I agreed to go out with him in the first place is that he plans to stay in the Atlanta area. Because I want to live and work here also, it's sensible not to get involved with anyone who intends to take a job out of state and move away.

One of the very few good pieces of advice Momma has ever offered was, "Don't date someone you wouldn't marry." Her reasoning is that you never know who you might fall in love with. That's not the part that worries me. I'm not even sure "falling in love" is an actual *thing*.

I just don't think it's logical to spend what little time I have outside of school and work with someone with whom there is no chance of a future. What's the point? I have plenty of female friends I can hang out with if what I want is to have fun. If I'm going to date, then it's got to have a good, solid reason behind it, or it's just not worth my time.

"So, can I tempt you with dessert?"

I grin at my solid, sensible, un-tempting date. "Sure. Why not?"

CHAPTER THREE
SCIENCE OFFICER

"I don't think you'll have any trouble with the live truck," Frank assures me at the station the next day. "I mean—you can *fix* the damn things, so I'd expect you can run an uplink for the six o'clock live shot."

I nod and follow as my boss slowly makes his way across the parking lot to the live truck. "Okay. If you say so. And that's all I have to do, right? Cause I've never used a news camera or anything before."

"That's it. Though you'll probably be fixing one of *those* tomorrow—the damn cheap ones they buy now have all kinds of problems. We've got three out of commission."

I wish I *was* staying at the station to work on camera problems down in the "engineering dungeon," as Frank calls it. I like it down there in the station's basement. It's quiet, filled with neatly arranged tools, and perhaps best of all, there's a complete Star Trek video collection.

In fact, that's what sealed the deal for me when I came in for an interview. Episode nineteen of the original series was playing at low volume on a monitor in the room when I arrived. When I mentioned it, Frank told me he owned the DVD's of every episode and played them all throughout the workday as background noise.

"Would you mind?" he asked.

"When can I start?" I responded.

Star Trek is like my meditation music. Growing up, I watched every episode with my dad over the years, while Momma and Kenley practically held their noses and ran away at the first bars of the theme song. That was fine with me. I liked that Daddy and I had our own little thing.

Star Trek and Elvis Presley will always and forever remind me of him. The fact that Frank enjoyed having the show play in the background as he worked made me feel instantly at home.

Another plus—the dungeon is far away from the bustling news department. I can't take all that craziness. I had to pass through the newsroom a couple times today, and both times Blake was there, offering me a big smile and trying to engage me in conversation. Unsuccessfully. I skittered away like some little furry creature surprised by the kitchen light coming on at two a.m.

I'm not sure why, but I don't want to talk to him. He's just so... so... actually, I don't know *what* he is since I barely know him. All I know is when Blake's around, I can barely think of a word to say, which is too weird. After a lifetime as Momma's second daughter, I've learned to be pretty handy with a comeback.

Frank unlocks the truck and opens the door, tapping a console inside. "Okay, so this is where you're gonna monitor your signal. And this is the hydraulic switch to raise and lower the mast—that's real important."

"Yes. I remember."

"Now, the photog and the reporter are gonna be outside the truck, close by. You've gotta make sure their shot is set up and coming in clearly ten minutes before their slot. If it's not there, the director's gonna tell the producer to float their story. And I'll let you in on a little secret—Leslie ain't fond of floating."

"Oh. Okay. Got it."

I met Leslie during the first few days of my internship. She's the six p.m. producer and without a doubt the boss of her show. She has this soft, almost cartoon-kitty kind of voice, but I've seen her make a huge editor cower after he made a sloppy mistake, and all the reporters seem to respect her. I said a quick hello and got the hell out of her way, which is where I've stayed. I definitely don't want to take the chance of disappointing her and joining the editor in the no-no corner tonight.

"So, walk me through the setup steps again," I say to Frank, and we both squeeze into the truck's narrow interior for a last-minute cram session.

Feeling a bit nervous but ready, I drive the truck to the live shot location—easy to find because it's right next door to the World of Coke, where I've been before. The live shot tonight is from the Georgia Aquarium. The world's largest aquarium is marking its anniversary, and there's a week-long celebration with special events and giveaways. I'm kind of thrilled this is my first live shot to go on, because it's pre-planned.

If they threw me out there on breaking news like a multiple shooting or something, I'd have less time to set up and even *more* nerves. But this should be simple and straightforward. There's no rain, and thanks to the "working press" sign on my dashboard, I get a good parking spot near the entrance of the aquarium.

I'm guessing the reporter—I think they said it was going to be Caroline—will stand somewhere out here with the boat-shaped curved glass exterior wall in the background, do her intro and then throw to the package of interior video and sound bites she's been gathering the past couple of hours. Now that I'm in place, all I can do is wait for her and the photog to emerge from the building. Then I'll stay out of their way as they edit the package in the truck before I set up the live shot.

While I wait, I sit in the driver's seat and drink a Pepsi One, glancing up guiltily at the monstrous Coca Cola sign towering above me, and try not to think of how Blake towered over me when we spoke briefly this morning. I hadn't thought it possible, but he smelled even better than he had yesterday, and those dimples were once again on full, mesmerizing display.

As if my memory has conjured him, the aquarium doors open, and Blake emerges. He's followed closely by Lucero Abrego, the only female photog working at WATV. *Blake?* What happened to Caroline?

The caffeine from my soft drink kicks in suddenly, or maybe it's the prospect of spending a couple hours in close proximity to Blake that's caused my pulse rate to double. That's the other apparent side effect of being near him. Tongue-tied and arrhythmic. Lovely combo.

He holds the door wide to let his co-worker pass. Luce is a teensy little thing, no taller than five-three with the frame of a ninth grader, but she seems super-capable, and from what I can tell, doesn't take any crap from the other photogs, though they seem to enjoy ribbing her.

We met on my first day during my "official" newsroom tour and talked a few minutes about the camera she uses. Turns out she's only a couple years older than me, and she's become my best friend at the station. We have lunch together most days unless she's out on a noon live shot or a story. As awkward as I find it to talk to Blake, chatting with Luce comes easily.

I can tell when the two of them spot the station-logoed truck. The pace of Blake's long stride picks up, and Luce almost skips to keep up with him, seeming unhindered by the camera on one shoulder and the equipment bag over the other. Blake's got his hands full, too, gripping a large duffle on each side.

When they get close, I climb into the back of the truck to open the side door for them. That's where all the editing equipment is, the place where they'll set up shop in preparation for their live shot. It's like a little mini TV station back here, with monitors, editing equipment, even a couple of wheeled office chairs so the reporter and photog can sit while they work.

I hear Blake's deep voice just outside the truck, and a ripple of awareness goes through my caffeine-or-whatever-addled-nervous system. Then I open the door to let them in.

His face is the first one I see, as little Luce's is somewhere down around my knees. His expression transforms from an easy smile into surprise, and then a distinct look of pleasure.

"Cinda. I didn't know you were our live truck operator today."

"I didn't either. I mean… uh… I *did* know I'd be running the truck. I didn't know I'd be yours. Your engineer I mean."

"Hi Cinda," Luce chirps. "How's it going? Big day for you— maiden voyage in a live truck, right?"

"Yeah. I'm hanging in there. How are you? How'd the shoot go?" I extend a hand to help her make the giant step up into the high profile vehicle, and she grabs it.

"Great. We got some great stuff for the package. Good thing you're here early though, because setting up *this* live shot's gonna be a bitch."

I look at her and then at Blake, who's joined us in the tiny central aisle of the live truck, keeping his head ducked so it doesn't crack the ceiling.

He's wearing an enthusiastic grin. "It won't be that bad. And it'll be so worth it—this live shot will be unprecedented."

I don't like the sound of this. This sounds hard. I was counting on straightforward. Where I come from, unprecedented and straightforward don't live in the same neighborhood.

"What... what are you planning to do?"

Luce rolls her dark brown eyes and blows a stray lock of black hair from her face. "Our new reporter is obsessed with creating the *ultimate* live shot."

"That's how we get to the network," he says in a teasing, instructive tone.

"Who's *we*, kimosabe? I like it fine just where I am. You go on ahead and chase stories around the globe. I'll just stay here in the greatest city in the world, drink my Coke, watch my Braves, and visit my fishies." She extends a hand in the general direction of the aquarium.

"I like the fishies, too. That's why I'm going to swim with them on live TV."

"You're going to do *what*?" I nearly shriek. "But you're doing the live shot out here, right? Outside the building?"

Blake gives me a naughty grin as he shakes his head in a definitive *no*. "Under. Water." He reaches into the bag and pulls out a wetsuit then a gigantic pair of swim fins, all of it bearing the Georgia Aquarium logo.

"But how? I mean... it's impossible... right? We don't have enough cable to reach the building."

Blake's confident smile never drops. "One of the biggest tanks is near the exterior wall in the back. They said you could park in the alley behind the building and lay cable through the emergency door there, since they've just closed for the night. We'll have a PR 'escort'—"

"Guard," Luce corrects.

"Right. A guard will open the door for us, and the truck won't be any further away from our shot location than usual."

"It makes more sense to do it right here—we've got a great backdrop of the aquarium—nothing can go wrong with the shot," I argue.

"Yeah, but it's so much *cooler* to do it in the fish tank."

Blake's cheeks dimple to their fullest mind-bending capabilities. *Must. Concentrate.*

"What about your microphone? You know you can't just put one of our mics in a Ziploc bag and use it underwater right? Sound transmission in water is totally different from sound in air. You'd need a hydrophone made from piezoelectric materials to convert the underwater sound waves into an electrical signal and feed it into an external speaker system or recording device, and…"

My voice trails off as I catch Blake's bemused expression and realize I've gone full-blown engineering geek on him.

He gives an exaggerated shrug, a smile tucked in one corner of his mouth. "Yeah. I knew that." And the rascally smile is joined by a glint of mischief in his green eyes. "I'm sure you'll figure it out, Spock. You *are* the science officer aboard this vessel."

I freeze in surprise at his Star Trek reference. Is he mocking me? Does he somehow know about my Trekkie tendencies? Studying his guileless face, I decide no, he doesn't know any more about me than I've told him.

At least he didn't call me Uhura. As far as the crew of the Starship Enterprise is concerned, he's pegged me just right. I always *wanted* to be Mr. Spock, so smart, so sensible, always sure of the right course of action. Logical. And not prone to irrational statements and fits of wild emotion like my mom.

I decide to take it as a compliment. "Okay. Whatever. Since we don't *have* a hydrophone handy, I guess we can leave a stick mic on the pool deck just outside the tank. You'll have to surface and grab it and start delivering your live lead-in. But if you drop it in the water—*you're* going to explain it to Frank. I want to go on the record as saying this is a *bad* idea."

Blake pauses for a second before agreeing in an undeterred tone. "All right. Duly noted and recorded."

The two of them stay in the back while I get into the driver's seat and maneuver the truck into the alley Blake indicates. As promised, a door is propped slightly ajar. Luce gets out and takes her camera and tripod inside to set up while I begin pulling cable from a giant spool inside the truck, dragging it up a short flight of concrete steps and through the back door of the building. The security guard, a large middle-aged woman in a dark uniform, nods to me and holds the door a bit wider.

Once her camera is secured on the tripod and connected to the cable, Luce goes back to the truck to begin editing the package with Blake. I take a few moments to explore my surroundings and gauge the challenges we'll face shooting in here. I grumble to myself, thinking of Blake's naughty-little-boy expression as he'd informed me of his intention to shoot underwater. And the delighted gleam in his eye as I warned him how difficult this was going to be. I think it actually made him *more* determined to pull it off.

He has to do it the hard way, doesn't he? Go for the big impact. If I'm Spock, then he's Captain Kirk, with all his swagger and charm. And recklessness.

I stroll the length of the room. I've been here before, years ago on a school field trip. It's quiet and dim, the low lighting provided by small canister lights in the ceiling high overhead. Some illumination also comes from the tank itself, which forms one whole wall of the room, at least two stories high and sixty feet wide. Directly opposite from the glass wall, stadium style risers provide seating for those who might want to sit and watch the assortment of marine life for a while.

At the moment it's empty and almost eerily quiet, since the exhibits closed at five p.m. I check my phone—5:30. Not much time to get everything ready. I need to have the shot up and looking perfect by 6:05, ten minutes prior to our 6:15 time slot, just before the weather segment. If I don't, the director will tell Leslie she has to float the shot, and she'll tell *me* to go to Hell probably. *Without* a paycheck. I can't start my part of the process until my counterparts are finished editing, so I study the room, imagining how the shot will go.

There's a staircase just to the left of the enormous tank, leading to an overhead observation area that allows aquarium visitors to view the fish from the top and the sides. If Blake begins his live shot underwater, Luce will have to start shooting down here on the floor then climb the stairs during the segment and follow him as he makes his way to the top of the tank. By the time he breaks the surface, she'll need to be at least even with him or above him in the observation area. I hope she's as good as I think she is. And has excellent balance.

I take a seat on the carpeted steps and watch the tank's inhabitants drift by, oblivious to the problems of a news station intern and the fact that their peaceful home is about to be invaded by lights, camera, *idiot*.

A school of small yellow fish suddenly speeds up and darts away toward the center of the tank. Then I see why. A large brown shark, about ten feet in length, swims close to the window. I shiver at the sight of its two back fins and tiny, soulless eyes.

Great. My first live shot and my reporter's *literally* going to get eaten alive.

CHAPTER FOUR
BAIT

I speed walk out to the truck and climb into the front seat, turning around to face Luce and Blake, who are huddled close in the back. They're both watching the monitors as she edits at lightning speed and he weighs in on sound bites and video choices.

"You might want to re-think this, cowboy. Did you know there are sharks in that tank?"

Blake lifts his head and laughs. "Only nurse sharks. They *rarely* bite humans."

"Oh, only rarely. That's good. Are you trying to get me kicked out of my internship your first week of work?"

"Are you kidding? The news director will love it—a shark attack will make for a way more exciting B-block, right?" Reading my scowl, Blake adds, "Relax. I'll have a dive escort with me, and the tour guide said nurse sharks are pretty laid-back." He hooks a thumb toward his chest and raises a suggestive eyebrow. "Besides, they don't like the *big fish*. They mainly eat small fish and shrimp—their favorite is lobsters."

"I recommend a hat then," I gesture to his red hair.

He nods with a half-grin. "Touche."

"Lighting's going to be a challenge," I warn Luce. "You can't use the stand lights while he's underwater—they'll reflect off the glass and give you nothing but glare, but you'll need light when he surfaces. It's dark in there."

She glances up from the editing console, her face twisted in dismay. "You're right. I'll shoot him through the tank window with no additional lighting and leave the stand light up at the top of the stairs, so it's on him when he comes up for air. I'll just have to put it in the right place so I don't hit it or cast a shadow when I'm climbing the stairs during the shot with my camera on my shoulder. And Blake, you're gonna have to keep your eye on me so our paces are even and we both reach the top at about the same time."

"*Assuming* Jaws doesn't get him first and he makes it at all," I mutter, twisting to check the time on the dashboard clock. "Twenty minutes till air. I need to raise the mast soon and see if we can even get a shot out of this canyon between the building and the parking garage. And you two should probably practice a couple of times. Y'all almost done?"

"Almost," Luce says.

At the same time Blake says, "Twenty minutes? Shit."

Hearing the sound of rustling, I turn back around and see Blake stripping. Yes, literally stripping off his clothes right there in the live truck.

He lifts his shirt over his head in one swift move, revealing an unexpected and rather delicious set of defined abs and a nice chest to go with them. His arms are long and well-muscled, and his lean waist is punctuated at either side by those Appollo's belt indentations that disappear under the waistline of his pants and make it impossible to stop imagining where they might lead.

Luce's gaze is lasered in on the monitors—either she's so focused on getting the story done by deadline that she doesn't notice the Chippendale's show behind her, or maybe this tempting sight is something she's already seen before? *Could they be... but no, he just started here.*

"Please. Feel free to watch," Blake's voice is teasing and seductively low as he reaches for the top button of his jeans.

I whip around to face the windshield. My face is mid-summer-in-central-Georgia-hot, and my voice sounds a little shaky when I speak. "*What* are you doing?"

"Well I can't put the wetsuit on *over* my clothes. I figured I'd better get started—don't know if you've ever worn one before, but these things aren't exactly easy to get on."

The chime of a text message interrupts him. There's movement in the rearview mirror as he reaches for his phone. Oh God. *The mirror.*

"Oh—my dive escort is already in the water waiting for me. I've got to get a move on," Blake says.

My mind barely registers his words, because now that I've caught sight of him in the mirror, I can't look away. I should. I have to.

But I just can't.

I can't see his eyes, (so I know he can't see mine) but I've got a great shot of him from the jaw down. He's managed to get the tight wetsuit up over his slim hips—thank God because it would be hard for him to do a live shot with a passed-out live truck operator. The suit clings to every hard-carved muscle of his thighs as well as the impressive topography between them.

As he works to inch the neoprene over his arms and back, his abs are performing all kinds of fascinating contortions. It's like I'm one of those characters in a kids' cartoon, mesmerized by an undulating cobra in a basket. His skin sliding over those delicious muscles is surprisingly tan for a redhead, sort of a golden color, and I feel the strangest urge to reach up to the mirror and stroke it.

"Done." Luce's victorious announcement brings me out of my trance and re-starts my lung function.

"Me, too," Blake says.

A loud *ZIP* punctuates his statement and signals the end of the show, but my body's not nearly done experiencing it. My pulse is still sprinting, nerve endings crackling, and my brain's not exactly in *engineering* mode. That'll have to change, because I don't have that much time left to get the shot up.

Suddenly Blake's face is close to mine, nearly cheek-to-cheek as he leans forward into the cab of the truck. "Are you ready?" he whispers, and the fruity gum smell of his breath joins with the light touch of whatever pheromone-laden cologne he's wearing to further unnerve me.

My instinct is to turn my face toward him, but that would put my lips in direct contact with his cheek, so I keep my head stock still, facing forward. "R-ready for what?" I stammer, barely able to keep my synapses firing enough to speak, much less decipher his meaning.

He leans back (thank you God) and says, "To get that shot up. You can do it, Spock. We're counting on you."

When I whip my head around to look at him, he's wearing his devilish grin and grabbing for the swim fins with one hand and the truck's door handle with the other. He opens the door and heads for the tank.

Luce rises from the stool she's occupied for the past twenty-five minutes and says, "Okay. Heading in there. Talk to you on the headset. Wish us luck."

"Okay," I wheeze, still recovering from my close encounter with Blake, "Good luck."

I take a minute to breathe, refocus and let the blood go back to my brain where I need it. Then I climb into the back of the truck and start setting live shot coordinates and communicating with the director in the station's control booth. Thankfully, I do manage to get a straight shot at the satellite, in spite of the high structures nearby, and the picture looks good back at the station. I still don't know if Luce and Blake can pull their part off, but if not, at least their failure will come in crisp and clear for all the viewers. I've done all I can do on my end.

On the preview screens in the truck, I watch them conduct several practice runs. It looks like my reporter and photographer will manage to arrive at the top of the tank simultaneously. Now, if Blake can swim to the correct spot, pick up his mic and deliver his lines without dropping the four hundred dollar device to the bottom of the tank, we'll be in good shape.

6:15 rolls around, and in my headset I hear the anchor begin reading the intro to our live shot.

"The Georgia Aquarium is celebrating its..." As he talks, the director takes Luce's camera. Then she's on the move, ascending the tank-side staircase, smoothly following Blake's figure through the clear glass wall as he kicks his fins, swimming for the surface. The low lighting actually works, creating a dreamy vibe. It doesn't hurt that he's surrounded by brilliant fish, who wriggle and dart past the lens in an underwater rainbow and generally treat their television debut like just another day in the tank.

And then the camera reaches the observation deck, Blake's head breaks the surface of the pool, and he swings it to the side to shake off the water. He smiles and rakes his wet hair back off his forehead. His other hand grasps the mic. "That's right, Ian, as you can see, I'm really getting *into* the Aquarium's anniversary celebration…"

He finishes his lead-in and tosses to the package without a hitch, as if he does live shots all the time while treading water and being nibbled by curious sea-creatures. Not only does he seem completely comfortable, he also looks good doing it. Like *really* good.

If I tried something like that, I'd resemble a drowned rodent with bad hair, red eyes and a sniffling nose, but Blake looks like one of those cologne ads where the male model is just emerging from a sparkling pool to show off his incredible physique and arresting eye color.

With his hair pushed away from his face, his bone structure really shows—the dimpled chin and broad cheekbones even more noticeable than usual. I'm tempted to ask for his parents' email address so I can congratulate them on the remarkable DNA combination they managed to achieve.

Blake finishes his lines, and the director takes the package Luce edited. I hear her and Blake asking each other how they think it went.

I hit the button to speak into her headset. "It looked good from here."

She passes the message on to Blake, who gives a Vulcan split-fingered hand sign to the camera instead of a thumbs-up. My face heats in a flush of unexpected delight. I'm sure the people in the director's booth are wondering what the heck it was for, but I know exactly what he's saying—*told you so, Spock.*"

The package will run about a minute and a half then Blake will have thirty seconds or so to do his live wrap and toss it back to the anchor. Hearing the last few sentences of the package, Luce refocuses the camera, and Blake picks up his mic from the pool-side surface. We're almost home.

Something moving along the water's surface behind Blake's left shoulder catches my eye. It's a fin.

Oh my God. It's a double-fin, and it's getting closer to Blake. I *knew* it. I push the headset button.

"Luce—tell Blake to get out of the water right now."

"What?" she responds. "We're almost back live. He's got to sig-out." Clearly she's too busy focusing on what's in her viewfinder to see what's about to *swim* into view and eat her reporter.

My voice goes up an octave and several decibels. "Look behind him. He needs to get out. Now."

I hear the sharp intake of her breath, then her panicked voice. "Blake—get out. Get out of the water—the shark—"

In response, he glances back over his shoulder. He shrugs and smirks at the lens. "Nah. It's fine. It's not going to hurt me. We're on in ten seconds."

Idiot. "Get him out, Luce," I order.

"Blake." Her plaintive whine seems to have no effect on him, except maybe to egg him on.

His grin widens. And the director takes Luce's shot.

"As you can see Ian…" Blake says as the shark circles him, crossing quite visibly between him and the camera, "…the humans aren't the only ones around here who are doing their part to make this anniversary celebration a success. Some of the animals are also ready and willing to sink their teeth into all the preparations."

"And into you as well, it looks like." The anchor chuckles. "Think we'd better cut out of the live shot early, Blake? It's only the six o'clock hour—a little early for blood on television."

"Don't worry about that, Ian. I don't eat seafood, so she's safe," Blake quips back, wearing a cheeky grin. "However, I *am* getting a little pruny, so I'll sign out now. Reporting live from the Georgia Aquarium, I'm Blake Branham, WATV—hey! Whoa."

The newscast cuts away from Luce's shot just as Blake is bumped violently to the side. I hear Ian wondering aloud over Blake's safety just before I rip my headset off, jump to my feet, fling open the sat truck door, and hit the ground running toward the propped aquarium door.

I fly up the staircase and reach the top in time to see Blake pull his last fin from the water and stand up on the deck to shake his dive escort's hand.

"Thanks. Good thing you had your little poker handy there," he says.

The young woman, also wearing a wetsuit, and wearing it quite well I have to say, laughs. "No problem. I think she was just annoyed—not actually going in for a bite. But a good time to get out of the tank, nevertheless." Her gaze slides up and down, taking in the entire picture of Blake in neoprene. She gives him a flirty grin. "You're brave—most people would've been out of the water at the first glimpse of a fin."

He shrugs, looking abashed. "Nah—not brave, just—"

"Stupid." I finish the sentence for him, standing with my arms crossed. My heart is still slamming from my mad dash, and my fury at his daredevil behavior is only increased by seeing the little waterside *amour* between him and the curvaceous aquarium employee.

Blake spins around to face me. He holds his arms out to the side and glances down at himself to demonstrate the lack of teethmarks. "See? I told you. Nothing to worry about. I was fine."

Too angry to respond, I glare at him for a second longer then turn without a word and disconnect the cable from Luce's camera. I start wrapping it around my palm and elbow, jerkily gathering it in a loop as I descend the stairs and make my way to the exit door. Behind me, I hear Luce folding the heavy tripod and Blake continuing his chat with the diver girl.

Cable rolled, I stomp out to the truck and stow it in the back. Then I climb into the front seat and start the truck's engine, eager to get back to the station and away from Blake's presence. *Far away.*

I'd love to start driving and strand him here without his clothes, but Luce left some of her stuff in the truck, too. Also, it would be terribly unprofessional. Besides, he wouldn't stay stranded for long. I'm sure his *dive escort* would be eager to offer him a ride back to the station—or anywhere else he wanted to go.

Hmmph. I drop my chin to my chest then lean my head to one side and the other, stretching neck and shoulder muscles that have become tense and bunched in the past ten minutes. Starting a bit at the sound of the truck's back door opening, I hear Blake and Luce laughing and chattering excitedly.

"You were almost the catch of the day," she teases as she steps up into the truck.

"Nah. She would've taken one bite and spit me out—I'm not that sweet."

I glance back at them. Luce raises a brow playfully as she watches him step up into the truck. "I don't know about that— you look pretty tasty to me—what do you think, Cinda?" She shoots me a big come-play-along grin.

I don't feel playful. "I think the shark showed she has excellent culinary taste—I wouldn't bite him either," I growl.

Blake's grin is instant and wide. "You sure about that Spock? You look like you want to tear into *something.*"

"I have a name you know."

He nods. "That's right—you know what—you just *tried* to save my ass, and I don't even know your real name."

Luce slaps his arm. "You on-air people are so self-absorbed. Her name's Cinda, you jerk."

"No. I mean I knew *that*. What's your whole name?"

Why does he want to know? Is he planning to google me or something? Look up my number? The thought makes me nervous, so I say something stupid, which is becoming a habit around him. "Cinda Moran—or the *other* Moran Girl, as I'm known."

Blake blinks. He looks startled, and then his brows come together and he shakes his head. "What does that mean?"

Luce jumps in before I can say, "Never mind."

"She's got a beauty-queen big sister all the guys were hot for. She even stole Cinda's high school sweetheart—every girl's nightmare—that bitch."

"No," I correct. "She's not a bitch, and she didn't steal him. He just *wanted* her to—like every single guy we ever knew." *Good Lord, Cinda. Shut up.* Why am I squirting lighter fluid on a conversational forest fire?

Luce saves me by changing the subject. "Hey, a bunch of us are going to go out after work tonight. Want to join?"

I do. But I've promised to have dinner at my parents' condo, which holds about as much appeal as a forest fire... or swimming in a tank *full* of sharks. Momma is better these days than she used to be. But that isn't saying much. A yeast infection is better than an STD, but you don't really want either of them.

"I wish I could. I have to have dinner with my parents."

"Come by after that. These things usually go until about ten."

"Okay. I'll try."

"Give me your phone." Luce holds out her hand, and I give her the phone. She talks while punching buttons. "I'm putting in my number. There. I just called myself from your phone, so now I've got yours. I'll text you the address of the place, and you can let me know when you're on your way."

Although we're buddies at work, we've never done anything outside the station before. I need to study, but she's hard to say no to. I guess there's a reason a lot of the reporters let her knock on the doors when they're out on tough stories together.

"Maybe. If I can."

"I'll see you there," she says insistently as she steps out of the live truck followed by Blake, who's strangely quiet all of a sudden.

In fact, he doesn't even say goodbye.

CHAPTER FIVE
FUZZY RECEPTION

I'm almost ready to go by the time Kenley drags in from work.

"Hey. Hard day?"

"Ugh. You have no idea. These fashion people can be so difficult. I had to spend an hour on the phone with Giovanni Rocco's assistant today, assuring her we wouldn't use *harsh* lighting on the set when he came on. We used every soft filter we had, and he still wasn't happy. I don't think he would've been truly satisfied unless we'd used only candlelight in the studio. So vain."

"Sounds stressful. However, it does not get you out of going to Momma and Daddy's tonight, so don't even try."

"Don't worry. I wouldn't abandon you like that. And Larson's still coming, too."

"Thank God. He's like the ultimate camouflage. Momma won't even notice I'm there."

"True. Even better, you should find your *own* distraction and bring *him* over," she teases.

"Are you kidding? And give her the joy of seeing me paired up with someone? She doesn't deserve that much happiness. Besides, I don't know anyone that distracting."

But a burst of recent memory makes me a liar. I get a picture of Blake undressing in the live truck mirror, and the image is so vivid I feel my face flush in a wave of heat and color. Thankfully, Kenley's not looking at me—she's sifting through the day's mail on the counter.

She turns back to me. "Are you ever going to forgive her? Not that she deserves it, mind you."

"Momma and I are fine," I protest in a tone that I can tell doesn't convince Kenley at all. I've always envied her ability to forgive and forget. Our mother hurt her just as much over the years—I saw it happen.

But somehow she always seemed to find another bit of room in her heart, some reserve supply of mercy I wasn't born with apparently. When Momma threw herself at our feet a few months ago, acknowledging her awful behavior and promising to change, Kenley was actually moved and is apparently willing to give her a total do-over.

I'm not sure I can do the same. Momma and I aren't openly fighting, and I don't *hate* her. In fact, I can't seem to muster any emotion at all where she's concerned anymore. She's made one remark too many, and now our relationship rests more on obligation and civility than any sort of affection on my part.

The good news is—she can no longer hurt me. I guess the bad news, if it *is* bad, is that I basically feel indifferent toward the woman who gave birth to me. It's better than hate, right?

Kenley steps close, touching my arm lightly then letting her hand fall to her side. I look at her face. Nope, she didn't buy it even a little bit.

"Believe me, I understand. And I'm not thinking about her. It's just bad for *you* to drag around all that luggage. If you don't find a way to forgive her, you'll only be smuggling that crap into your future," she warns.

I lift my chin. "I'm fine. Anyway, I'll stop blaming Momma, as soon as *she* stops telling lies."

Kenley snorts a laugh. "You might as well wait for the sun to stop coming up every day. She's lied so often she barely even realizes the difference between her version of reality and the truth."

Throughout our entire childhoods, Momma put on airs and invented an entirely new background for herself in an effort to cover up a childhood marked by poverty and depravation. I used to feel so confused when she'd give a fictitious account of events I'd been present for. When I was old enough to figure out she was a habitual liar, the confusion shifted into embarrassment.

She only turned a corner recently after alienating me and Kenley and almost losing Daddy. I have to admit she *has* improved since then. She seems less materialistic and doesn't criticize us as often for failing to meet her particular expectations, but the exaggerations (lies), embellishment (lies), and wishful thinking (lies) have continued. I can hardly stand to be around her when she gets going.

"I think she's really trying," Kenley continues. "Daddy says she cancelled all her magazine subscriptions so she won't be as tempted to shop, and they're making progress toward getting the debt paid down."

"Well that's good. They don't have *room* for any new stuff now, anyway, even if they did have the money."

Kenley and I get into her car and drive to our parents' condo in Roswell, north of the city. As part of their "starting over" plan they sold their oversized home in the affluent neighborhood where we grew up in Alpharetta. She told her country club friends the house was just "too much" to take care of, what with all their extensive "travel plans." I've wondered if they noticed she sold most of her jewelry, too.

The condo is barely a quarter of the size our house was, but the atmosphere inside is a vast improvement. Daddy no longer seems so tense and overworked, and being with the two of them is overall more pleasant.

"We're here," Kenley calls out as she opens the front door with her key.

"In the kitchen, girls," Momma's voice sings out.

We walk down the tastefully appointed hallway and into the airy, open kitchen. Momma gives us bright smiles, rushing over to greet us each with a cheek kiss.

I watched *both* your shows today. I liked that Mr. Rocco, Kenley. He seems like a hoot."

"That's one word for him," Kenley replies with a grin.

"He looks so young. I can't believe he's in his sixties," Momma says.

"That makes two of you. He can't believe he's in his sixties, either. He also can't believe women in their early twenties aren't flattered to have his hands on their backsides."

"Oh dear. He made a pass at you?" Momma's newly-mobile-Botox-free brows actually *move* in an expression of disapproval. "Larson wouldn't like to hear that."

"Hear what?" A polished male voice booms from the foyer.

Daddy has obviously let Larson in. They round the corner together, and Larson's tall, athletic frame and handsome face come into view. Like Blake, Larson's a redhead. But while Blake's hair is a beautiful, deep auburn shade, my sister's fiancé has hair that's more on the strawberry-blonde side, reminding me of a young Robert Redford.

Daddy comes over to give me a hello and a cheek kiss, while Larson goes straight for Kenley, wrapping his arms around her in an enthusiastic embrace that pulls her to her tiptoes. After dropping a quick kiss on her lips, he asks, "Who made a pass? Do I need to go set someone straight at WNN?"

She laughs, obviously pleased by his possessiveness and his pretend threat. "No silly. Unless you're in the habit of roughing up elderly fashion designers. Your mom probably wouldn't appreciate it if you beat up her competitor—might look like sour grapes."

"I don't care who it is—he could be Ralph Lauren—nobody lays a hand on my girl... other than me." Larson gives her bottom a playful tap, then seems to finally notice there are other life forms in the room. "Hey Cinda. Hello Mrs. Moran."

"Hi Larson," I say, giving him a quick hug.

Momma bustles over and lifts her cheek for a kiss. "I keep telling you to call me Lisbeth. And I'm also telling you—you'd better hurry up and put *another* ring on it, Larson. Kenley's always had men falling at her feet. Better lock her down before she gets away."

"Lisbeth." Daddy's tone is low and calm and accompanied by a light squeeze to Momma's forearm as he steps up to her side. The man's work is never done—he sure has more patience than I do.

Momma yanks her arm away, and her face takes on that *okay, okay, I know* expression. Kenley shoots me a secret look, communicating what we're all thinking—Momma hasn't changed *that* much.

"What did you think of my live shot today?" I ask to change the subject from husband-to-be-hounding.

"Oh. The whole show was wonderful, darling. Now remind me, which live shot was yours?"

Nope. Things aren't that different. Momma has always been tuned into the Kenley Channel, even before her firstborn daughter got into TV news. Where I'm concerned, her reception has always been a bit fuzzy.

"The one at the aquarium, right pumpkin?" Daddy offers quickly.

I take a calming breath before answering. "Right. Remember the story where the reporter was in the fish tank?"

A look of recollection in my mother's eyes. "Oh yes. *He's* an attractive fellow."

To my mortification, my face heats in a full blush. I open the refrigerator and stick my head inside, pretending to look for a drink. "He's okay, I guess. Any Mountain Dew in here?"

"You know I only buy diet drinks. Too many liquid calories will catch up with you," she warns.

She's probably right—after all, her midlife figure is one many girls my age would envy—but I spend enough time running and playing lacrosse I'm not worried about indulging in the occasional sugary drink.

"Momma." Kenley's warning tone floats across the room.

During our family "intervention" Momma promised to cut out the weight-shaming of her daughters, and for the most part, she's been controlling herself. But the impulse is still in there.

It's probably second nature to her by this point, as her primary goal since our births was grooming us to meet and marry wealthy men. Making sure we maintained attractive figures was a vital part of that plan. Of course, Kenley, being the obedient and compliant child she was, followed the plan a whole lot better than I did—that was until her first engagement ended and she completely rebelled. She hooked up with Larson in *spite* of his money instead of because of it.

My own rebellion began at about age nine, when I adamantly refused to participate in any more Little Miss pageants and started coming home daily with my prissy, expensive school dresses mysteriously stained and shredded. Eventually she gave up and washed her hands of the whole business of trying to make me an *appropriate lady* and doubled-down on her efforts with Kenley— my poor sister.

"You didn't mention who you worked with today," Kenley says. "Who was the reporter?"

"His name's Blake."

"Oh, I love that name. I dated a guy in college named Blake."

Larson picks that moment to wrap an arm around his fiancée and pull her back possessively against his chest. Because he's behind her, Kenley can't see the slight downturn of his lips and the pinching of his brows—he obviously hates the thought she ever dated anyone before him.

She goes on without missing a beat. "So how was he? Some reporters can be hard to work with."

"He was… fine." I find myself not wanting to talk about Blake. "He did a good job. Almost got eaten by a shark, though."

We all sit down to dinner, and I tell the whole story, much to Larson's amusement. "I did some pretty out-there live shots during my time in local news… but I was never shark-bait."

"I wish I could've seen it." Kenley pouts. "I hate that my show is on at the same time as yours. I've never even seen the early evening news there. I'm going to start DVR'ing it now that you're going out on live shots."

I shrug, pausing in the act of lifting a forkful of salad to my mouth. "It's not like you can see *me* anyway—I'm just there behind the scenes."

"So am I these days. I'd still be able to recognize good work when I saw it."

"You must have done a great job—it looked flawless," my father says.

I give him a rueful smile. "Thanks Daddy. Now, if I can just find someone who agrees with you *and* pays before this co-op ends—I'll be in good shape."

"Any leads on a summer position yet?" Kenley knows my need for a paycheck as well as I do. She covers the lion's share of our rent, but it really helps when I can contribute. Momma and Daddy have their own financial issues to overcome, so counting on them for support isn't an option.

"Not yet. But I will soon. Don't worry."

"I'm not worried." She smiles.

Larson takes her hand. "You *know* you could both move in with me. I have plenty of room."

"I don't think so," I say immediately.

Kenley apes a black-and-white-movie Southern belle. "Why sir—we are *not* that kind of ladies, and you are *no* gentleman."

He grins and draws her closer, obviously delighted by her exaggerated chewy drawl. The desire in his eyes when he looks at her causes a twisting in my gut. Will someone ever look at me that way?

"I'm just ready to have you within arm's reach," he says. "Why do we have to wait until next spring to get married?"

"You know why—because your parents are planning the Wedding to End All Weddings, and their international guests need advance warning of this sort of thing." In a sweetly facetious tone she adds, "It would be *such* a shame if all those royals and celebrities weren't able to make it."

Kenley confessed to me she'd rather have a small ceremony with just family and close friends or even elope. All she cares about is spending her life with Larson, but she understands his parents' position on the matter, too. He's their oldest child, their only son, and they have a *lot* of friends who want to share the occasion. And from what I've heard about his younger sister Rory, his might be the only wedding the Overstreets ever get to plan—she's apparently doing her best to live up to the wild-child heiress stereotype and has given no indication of ever intending to settle down.

"Besides, I can't leave my roomie," Kenley adds, bumping my shoulder with hers.

"Thank you." Next spring I'll graduate, hopefully find a job immediately, and be able to support myself and pay my own rent. I'll never be able to thank Kenley enough for getting me out of my parents' house until then.

"Honey, you know you always have a place here—we have an extra bedroom and bath," Daddy says, after chewing the last bites of his meal.

Momma obviously loves that suggestion, and she rolls with it. "That's right, Larson. Cinda can come back and live with me and Kevin anytime, so if y'all want to move in together—go right ahead."

I doubt that was the point Daddy was making, and looking at his face, I see I'm right. He's red all the way up to his receding hairline. How does he put up with her?

Kenley just rolls her eyes at Momma's blatant pimping. Most proper Southern moms wouldn't push their daughters to cohabitate before marriage, but I guess Momma is going to stay terrified of losing her dream-come-true future son-in-law until the vows are said and the ink is dry.

"Well, thanks for the offer, but that won't be necessary," I say. I'm trying to keep it polite and calm.

"Especially if you hurry up and find your *own* man," Momma says. "You know, Mitzy said Mark isn't with anyone right now."

"Momma!" Kenley and I screech at the same time.

Only I continue, and *calm* is no longer an option. "You are *not* trying to set me up with Kenley's ex-fiancé—are you?"

She blinks a few times, drawing back into her chair. "Well… he's still a good catch, and he's from good stock."

"He *cheated* on me, Mother," Kenley reminds her. "Cinda's not interested in dating a cheater."

"And I'm not interested in dating anyone who dated Kenley. Or anyone whose *stock* you might be coveting."

She gives us a guilty smile. "It's not about the Fitzsimmons' money, truly. I was just thinking…"

"Good Lord, Lisbeth. We talked about this," Daddy growls as he gets up from the table and carries his empty plate to the sink. He drops it in and heads down the hallway toward the bedrooms, where I have a pretty good idea what he'll do—put in a DVD from his vast collection of classic Star Trek episodes—comfort food for the eyes and ears.

I stand to join him, not finished with my own dinner, but no longer feeling hungry and *definitely* over my limit on Mom-time. I'd rather hang out with Daddy and the crew of the Enterprise any day. "You know what Momma? Don't try to think of anyone for me, okay? I can manage my own love life."

Actually, I haven't had spectacular success in that department, but the last thing I need is *her* playing matchmaker for me. She wouldn't have any idea what kind of guy I'd like. And that she'd even consider setting me up with Kenley's ex… it just proves how little she knows me.

Doesn't Momma remember the disastrous end to my great high school love affair? How Tyler used me just to get close to Kenley, the *real* target of his affection? It was the last time I gave in to my recessive emotional side and abandoned myself to a day-long, illogical, indulgent weep-fest.

No—I don't have many criteria for the guys I date—but *not* being Kenley's sloppy seconds is at the top of my short list.

Also not on my list? Swaggering, risk-taking hellions with too much charm and off-the-charts testosterone counts. So why has Blake's face been coming back to my mind over and over again throughout the evening?

CHAPTER SIX
ROOFTOP RENDEZVOUS

My phone rings as Kenley and I get into the car to leave. She's driving me back home before grabbing her things and heading over to Larson's house for the night. She certainly *should* provide him with some company and whatever else he wants. Any man who'll hang out with our mother without being forced to by biological or marital bonds *deserves* a reward.

I swipe the answer button on the screen. "Hello?"

"Cinda—it's Luce. Where are you? Still at your folks'?"

"Just leaving."

"Good. Now get your ass over here. We're at 866 Rooftop. It's in Midtown." There's loud music in the background, and it sounds like fun.

"Oh. Is... everyone still there?" I'm embarrassed to realize the only part of "everyone" I actually want to know about starts with a *B* and ends with *lake*.

"Yeah. There's a lot of us. You could get to know some more of the news people." I hear a scraping noise and the sound of muffled voices as she apparently turns from the phone to talk to someone else. "Sorry. That was Blake. He wants to know if you're coming."

I hesitate as I'm swept up in a swirling butterfly tornado. "I'm… not sure. I have some studying to do… "

"You don't need studying—you need a watermelon margarita. Trust me. I'm a news photographer—I know what I'm talking about." She giggles. "I'm texting you the address, and I'd better see your little blonde head here soon."

"Who was that?" Kenley asks.

"My friend Luce from the station. She's the photog I worked with tonight. She's totally drunk."

"Well, you're going, right? It's important to make friends with the people at work. That's part of the intern experience."

"I don't know. Maybe." The thought of seeing Blake outside of work is equally compelling and terrifying. Especially if he really was asking about me.

"Take my car," Kenley says, as if it's a done deal. "Just don't *you* get drunk. Your career in news will be over before it starts if you get a DUI. And you do *not* want to get into a wreck in a Prius. The other car will win—trust me—I've covered too many ugly accident scenes in my news career."

"Don't worry. I won't."

While we're stopped at a red light, Kenley blows a kiss into the rearview mirror. I look behind us. Larson's there, following in his own car.

I turn back around and roll my eyes, smiling. "Y'all are ridiculous. Maybe you *should* just go ahead and elope."

She laughs brightly. "I'd love to, believe me. But when you find your true love someday, you'll understand—the right one's worth waiting for."

True love? I give a small, noncommittal grunt. I can tell Kenley's happy—happier than I've ever seen her before—but I'm not sure about the notion of true love, or that there's one for everyone.

There are plenty of people who never find someone like that, aren't there? There are those who think they have, and then a few years later change their minds. And what about all those old couples married for sixty-something years after wedding as teenagers? Did *love* really carry them through the decades or was it a *decision* on their parts?

I think it's the latter. Like my parents for instance—they married when my mom got pregnant with Kenley right after high school graduation. Then in spite of extreme duress, at least on my dad's part, they've gutted it out and stayed together all these years.

It seems to me the best thing you can do is make a wise, considered choice of partner, then decide to see it through. Unless you don't marry at all, which is a viable choice as well. I will eventually, or at least I want to, because I want to have kids someday. Besides, I'm not exactly motivated to have sex with a string of different guys throughout my lifetime. It's not even that great, so limiting it to one partner for life will at least be safe and sanitary.

Larson meets us in the parking lot of our complex, and Kenley hands me her keys. Thirty minutes later I step from the elevator onto the roof deck of 866 Rooftop. The bar area is packed. If it's this mobbed at nine o'clock on a Tuesday night, I can't imagine what the weekends are like. I glance down at myself—better than usual—yellow denim skirt, layered tank tops, sandals—but I still feel underdressed. This crowd is classy.

The open-air rooftop lounge itself is pretty swanky, too. There are white-curtained cabanas, glass-topped tables, and gorgeous landscaping with lemon trees and an herb garden. Low-slung comfortable chairs are placed around fire pits, while side tables hold sleek lanterns, adding to the glow. It's like being in an ultra-cool rooftop garden. The calm feeling of sitting out under the stars contrasts with the vibrant energy of the hip-looking crowd. Low murmurs of conversation are interspersed with the clinking of cocktail glasses, mixing with some kind of foreign-language house music.

I look around for familiar faces, but it's dark and there are so many people. Everyone kind of looks the same to me. Insecurity and a sudden craving for my pj's and cable TV swamp me. Before I can turn and get back into the elevator, I hear Luce's voice calling my name. She pops up from her chair and waves wildly from one corner of the deck.

"Hey! You came," she says when I make it to the fire pit area where about ten of my co-workers from WATV are lounging on plush green-cushioned outdoor sofas.

As I glance over the group, a shimmer of nerves hits my stomach. The loose waves of Blake's hair glint red in the light from the fire pit. I can only glimpse the side of his face. He's in animated conversation with a small brunette next to him—maybe the little owl from the assignment desk? The girl's face is blocked from my view by his wide shoulders. Are they flirting? I thought maybe he liked Luce. Maybe he likes *both* of them. With his looks and charm, he doesn't have to settle for one girl at a time.

When I step into the conversation circle, his focus turns to me. Heat sparkles across my skin as his gaze glides down my body in a slow inspection then snaps back to my face. His green eyes gleam with a wicked implication that makes my muscles clench from my core down to my toes, as if I'm struggling to keep my balance on this flat, unmoving surface.

Standing beside me, Luce slips an arm through mine and pulls my attention back to the rest of the group. "Y'all, everyone needs to buy Cinda a drink tonight," she announces to them. "She's our new resident live-shot guru. She's the one who pulled off the aquarium thing today."

A little cheer goes up.

"Spock!" Blake contributes at a loud volume, cupping his hands around his mouth like a megaphone.

I am the recipient of several congratulatory back slaps and high fives from the group, which includes Gabe, a morning reporter, who slides over to make room for me on his couch cushion. I recognize Caroline, the reporter I was expecting on our live shot, and Alissa, the baby owl girl—I was right—she *is* the one Blake was talking to—and a couple of photogs whose names I can't remember. There's a really young-looking editor named Chris I've spoken to a couple of times. The evening anchor, Ian Pence is also here, though I know he has to do the eleven tonight—I guess this is his dinner break.

I don't know any of them very well, but they all seem nice. Well, maybe not Ian—golden blond, sophisticated, and too handsome for his own good, he has a reputation as an alpha-hole womanizer—so I've made sure to keep my distance from him.

They must have all been here a while, since most of them seem well on their way to happy-drunk. Except for Ian, who has to stay alert for the late news. And Blake. His sharp-eyed perusal of me leads me to believe he is completely sober.

After I sit down, Luce takes a seat on Chris's lap. Okay, so *not* with Blake then...

I check his expression to make sure. All smiles. So *they're* not together, but I'm still not sure about the little pocket-pet beside him. Alissa's sitting awfully close, working hard to re-capture his attention. And who can blame her? He's still wearing his work clothes, slacks with a nice button-down, but he looks different now, sort of rumpled and relaxed with a couple buttons undone and wind-blown hair.

My eyes meet his, and I realize I've been staring. He gives me an alert glance that tells me he's noticed. My breath quickens, joining my now-hurried pulse, and I jerk my gaze away. It lands on Alissa's face. Which looks none-too-pleased.

"Anyone need a drink?" Without waiting for an answer, Blake stands. "I'm headed to the bar. What do you want, Cinda?"

"Oh—a beer. Light beer," I add, remembering my promise to Kenley. "Thanks." I start to pull some bills from my purse, but he waves the money away and heads for the bar.

I chat with Gabe, answering the usual questions about how school's going and how long I'll be staying at the station. In a few minutes, Blake comes back with a bottled beer for me and something that looks like cola for himself—maybe a mixed drink?

"Scoot," he orders, and squeezes in between me and Gabe, who was starting to tell me about the meth-lab bust story he covered last night. Apparently he was quite heroic, charging in alongside the police, wearing his own Kevlar vest and helmet.

"Hey—find your own seat, asshole." Gabe says.

"I just did. There's more room over there if you're crowded." Blake nods toward the spot he recently vacated next to Alissa.

Gabe gives him a hard look, which Blake meets with an unrepentant smile. Finally, Gabe harrumphs and stands, moving to the other side of the fire pit to take the empty seat. Alissa doesn't seem any happier than her new cushion-mate. She scowls in my direction before turning to respond to something Gabe has said to her. Maybe *she'll* be impressed by the meth lab story.

"So…" Blake's glass clinks against my bottle in a little cheers move. "Still mad at me?"

"I wasn't mad."

A wry smirk lifts one corner of his mouth, and his green eyes twinkle with amusement. "Yes you were. You thought I was taking stupid chances—"

I smile sweetly at him. "You *were* taking stupid chances."

"Okay, well yes. But I had a good reason for it."

"What's that?"

He leans in with a conspiratorial whisper, "I was trying to impress a girl."

I shiver in the warm night air. Which girl? Does he mean Diver Girl... *or me?* Because the way he's looking at me now with that wicked grin and one eyebrow expectantly raised makes me think it's the latter.

My fingertips dig into the seat cushion, and I swallow hard. The side of my neck feels like it has its own heartbeat. This guy has a real gift for knocking me off-balance. To cover, I search for a glib response.

Raising one eyebrow in my best imitation of Mr. Spock, I say, "That was foolish, Jim."

For a second Blake looks hurt that I've called him the wrong name. Then the understanding dawns on his face, and he laughs. "A fellow Trekkie, huh?"

"Yeah. My dad's a diehard fan. Yours too?"

He shakes his head and darts his eyes away. "Uh... no. My sister and I used to watch it after school every day." Now his gaze returns to me and brightens. "Anyway, I couldn't help myself. Don't you ever do anything *illogical*, just because it feels right?"

"No," I tell him honestly.

He nods. "Well I do. And maybe it *was* foolish, but maybe I was overwhelmed by *illogical* beauty." He gives me a look that erases all doubt as to which girl he was showing off for today.

The pulse in my neck is pounding harder. I reach up to cover it with my hand, shrugging to disguise my discomfort. "Well, I'm sure there were plenty of beauties out there in TV land who were very impressed by your bravery." *And your body in a skin-tight wetsuit.*

"But not you."

Still dwelling on the mental image of that wetsuit, I'm not really sure I heard what he said. "What?"

"I take it you weren't impressed. What's your major at Tech?"

I shake my head in confusion, trying to follow the quick shift in topic. "I'm double-majoring actually—in Mechanical and Industrial engineering."

He nods sagely. "Ah, just as I suspected."

"What?"

"You're way too smart for me," he says with a deep laugh.

I laugh, too, uncomfortable with his suggestion that he is in any way *for me*. "*You're* smart."

"No. I'm quick on my feet. There's a difference. I got totally mediocre grades—and that was just journalism school."

A breeze blows a lock of his reddish-gold hair over his forehead, and he lifts a hand to rake it back.

Suddenly, I have a suspicion that turns the beer in my stomach into ice. Kenley, who's always had a thing for redheads, mentioned having a former boyfriend named Blake—another journalism major at University of Georgia. It's a common enough name in the South, but still...

I work to keep my question from sounding like an enemy interrogation. But the response he gives will be critical. "Where did you go to J-school?"

"Oh, I uh... graduated from Kennesaw State."

Blake looks almost embarrassed at the admission, but I'm beyond relieved. If this *was* Kenley's Blake, I'd have to stand up and walk off no matter how adorable he looks in his after-work unbuttoned style.

Now that I'm no longer worried about being a consolation prize to Kenley's first choice again, I'm curious about Blake's reaction to my simple question. Kennesaw is a smaller state school, but it has a good reputation. So I'm not sure why he would act strangely about it. He seemed... evasive.

I don't like evasive. After a lifetime of my mom's casual and sometimes damaging lies, I crave complete and utter honesty.

"So... you didn't like it there?"

He hesitates, starts to speak and stops, then starts again. "It was fine. It turned out to be... the best place for me."

Clearly, this is not his favorite topic. Though I'm still curious about his hesitance, I decide to drop it and ask about another aspect of his past. "Play any sports in school?" He has the build of an athlete for sure.

His eyes study mine, boring into me as if trying to discern some purpose for my asking beyond mere curiosity. His face is tight when he finally answers. "Yeah. I played baseball in high school and a couple years in college, but I injured my elbow and had to quit."

"Oh. I'm sorry. That had to suck."

"Yeah. It did. I lost my scholarship." And he stops there.

And... apparently we're done with that topic, too. A few awkward moments pass as I wonder how to get the conversation back on the rails and figure out where things went wrong. Blake seems to be doing the same thing.

We start speaking at the same time, "You know..." he says, then stops. "Sorry. Go ahead."

"No, that's alright. You go."

"I was about to say… it wasn't all bad, you know, losing my scholarship. It made me get more serious about school. I started treating it like a job and just focused on getting out of there and getting my career started."

Wow. He's just expressed my precise attitude toward collegiate life. I haven't met too many people who don't think of it like a four-year party. I nod excitedly. "I know exactly what you mean. My sister just today warned me about never having any fun in college. But I don't really have time for fun, you know? I have a brutal course load, and I work…"

He studies my face a moment, his eyes glinting with devilry. "So then… you really have *no* time for anything fun… at all? Cause I was kinda hoping you'd go out with me sometime." He holds up his hand in a placating gesture. "If you like, I can guarantee there's no actual fun involved."

In spite of the sharp reverberation through my nerves, or maybe because of it, I laugh out loud. "Oh really? How can you make sure I won't have fun? What would we do on this no-fun date?"

Blake leans back on his hands and squints up at the night sky, contemplating. "Hmmm. I could take you to the dump—no that's actually kind of interesting, seeing all the things people throw out. Let's see… oh I know. We could get out on 285 in the middle of rush hour—no that might be fun with you as well—although the air conditioner in my truck needs freon, so maybe that's back on the table."

"Sounds promising," I agree, then make my own suggestion. "You could force me to sing karaoke."

"You don't like karaoke?"

"*Hate* it. I can't sing at all. My mom used to put me in these little-kid beauty pageants, and I swear it was all the judges could do not to plug their ears during my *talent* segment."

He laughs and makes two check marks on an invisible list in the air. "Karaoke, beauty pageants. How else may I torture you and keep my promise of no fun? Take you to a NASCAR race?"

"No. Those actually *are* fun. Ever been to one?"

"Never. But *now* I can't take you to one because you *like* it."

"We could go visit my mother," I joke, literally shuddering at the thought of bringing a guy home to her and the way she'd undoubtedly rip Blake for his lack of personal wealth.

"Or mine," he mumbles, and then he flushes deeply, looking away as if wishing he hadn't said it.

I lean toward him, nudging his shoulder playfully with mine to lighten the mood again. "I wouldn't mind meeting your mom, seeing all your little carrot-top baby pictures."

"Yeah, um, *that's* never gonna happen." Blake stands, pulling a set of car keys from his pocket while looking out over the skyline. "It's getting late."

Okay, well I guess the party's over.

"I should head out, too, I think. I have class in the morning." As I rise to join him, I sway backward a bit from standing too quickly.

One of his large hands wraps around my bicep, steadying me. "Hey, you okay to drive? Want me to give you a ride?"

"No, I'm fine. I only had the one—"

"*I* need a ride. I'm drunk off my ass," Alissa blurts loudly, also coming to her feet.

True to her word, she rocks back and forth like a sapling in a stiff wind. She stumbles toward us, nearly careening into the fire pit, and comes to a stop right next to Blake. She clenches her skinny arms around his midsection.

"Can you drive me, Blakey?" She gazes up at him like an adoring child then turns her sharp little nose toward me. "He's our designated driver. He's a good boy, aren't you, Blakey?"

She pats his flat stomach familiarly then lays her head against his chest. Her eyes settle on me and narrow with a challenging spark. Suddenly, she doesn't seem quite as drunk.

Ignoring her, I ask Blake. "You didn't drink tonight?"

Wearing a look of unmistakable distaste, he extricates himself from her death lock and turns back to me. "No. I uh… didn't want anything. You sure about that ride?"

"Totally. And I've got to get my sister's car home. I should probably drive Luce home, too. So, I guess I'll see you at work."

"Sure, but listen—"

Alissa grabs his hand, pulling him and giggling. "Come ooonnn, Blakey," she whines.

He tosses her an annoyed glance. "In a minute, Alissa, *hold on.*" Turning back to me, he says, "So listen… what do you think? About what I said earlier?"

I pause, considering it. I'm definitely tempted, because I have a feeling whatever we'd end up doing, we *would* have fun. But I'm not sure I should say yes to a date with Blake. He doesn't make sense for me. He's years older, has ambitions to work at the network, which will take him away from Atlanta eventually. He wasn't exactly forthcoming about his past when I asked, and I hate secrets. Plus, he is *such* a Kirk, light-years away from the betas and *Ensign Jim's* I've been dating since starting college.

So I don't answer. "Looks like you've got all the *fun* you can handle there tonight. See you tomorrow, Captain."

Wrapping herself around him again, allegedly for support, Alissa pulls Blake away from me. "I'm *so* tired. You may have to carry me," she slurs.

With a frustrated sigh, Blake allows himself to be led toward the elevator exit, and I start saying my goodbyes to the group. I'm offering a ride to Luce, still watching Blake and Alissa's departure from the corner of my eye, when I catch the top of his auburn head over the crowd.

He's turned to look back over his shoulder. And I think he's looking for me, because when our eyes meet, he gives me a huge, dimpled smile and lifts one hand in a high wave. Then he whips around and catches Alissa, narrowly saving her from tripping and falling on her sneaky little fake-drunk butt.

CHAPTER SEVEN
TWO OFFERS

When I get to work and go down to the basement the next morning, I'm struck by the scent of roses. Reaching the engineering office I see why—I mean, I can't miss them. The arrangement is huge, hot pink blooms spilling over the sides of a gorgeous, cut-glass bowl that's sitting right on the work table.

For a second my heart seizes, and I think of Blake. *No, that's silly.* These have to be for someone else. Maybe they were meant for one of the anchors or reporters upstairs in the newsroom?

I walk over to the table. There's a card. Still convinced the flowers are here by mistake, I reach for the little envelope. And my name's written on the outside.

Now my heart is pounding like I've got a migraine in my chest. I drop the envelope on the table, then immediately feel silly. *It doesn't contain anthrax, Cinda.* I pick it up again and lift the little flap to pull out the card inside. And drop that.

"Looking forward to having no fun with you..." is all it says.

The pulmonary migraine intensifies. This is... this is weird. And *romantic*. And though in movies I laugh at stuff like this, I'm not laughing now. I'm sort of hyperventilating, truth be told.

No one's ever sent me flowers before. There was the dyed carnation wrist corsage Tyler gave me for prom and the single rose Troy handed me the other night at the start of our date. But no one's ever had a whole bouquet delivered.

I lean in and sniff the sweet perfume of the roses, and it only increases the swirling sensation in my belly. What does it mean? I guess he didn't end up in an inebriated booty call with Alissa last night, a thought which pleases me more than it probably should. Unless he's such a player that he was kissing her and texting his florist order at the same time. But I don't think that's who he is.

And so I'm a complete and utter mess for the rest of the morning. I hide in the engineering dungeon, half-hoping Blake will show up at the door and half-hoping he's called in sick today.

The thought of seeing him excites me, but I need some more time. I need to think about this whole thing logically, to go back over the pros and cons list I made at around midnight last night. But I *can't* think.

I hardly slept, and when I did, it wasn't good sleep—short periods of unconsciousness broken up by frequent dreams of a red-haired, dimpled baseball player, sharks, and worst of all, Karaoke. My singing hadn't improved a bit, not even in my dreams.

I work on a malfunctioning news camera, enjoying the relaxation afforded by simple things like CMOS sensors and image stabilizers. Fixing camcorders is easy—it's relationships that are hard.

About fifteen minutes prior to the noon newscast, I'm called up to the director's booth. The switcher isn't working properly, and Frank wants me to watch him work on it, so I'll know what to do if it happens again while he's not in the building. Without the studio live switcher, the newscast would consist of a single camera shot instead of the two or three you'd normally see over the course of a half hour show.

I'm shining a flashlight on the underside of the equipment, watching Frank jiggle first one wire then another, when a raspy baritone voice comes through the monitors in the booth, startling me and giving me instant goose bumps.

"Three, two, one... mic check. Coming up today at noon... a routine shark attack goes horribly wrong." Blake's deep laugh follows his silly made-up news tease, and the audio board operator chuckles.

She glances over at me. "He makes up a new one every day. It's always 'a routine drive-by shooting' or 'a routine nuclear attack'—something like that. Yesterday, it was 'a routine F-5 tornado goes horribly wrong.'" She chuckles again and shakes her head, hitting a button so that Blake hears her in his IFB. "Okay honey, you're good."

I look up at the screens lining one wall of the small room, and there's Blake, in beautiful hi-def living color. He's in the studio, getting ready to do a live intro for his story on the noon news. The studio camera op zooms in tight to focus, and Blake's gorgeous light green eyes fill the screens. God, who looks that good in super-close-up? Even his pores are beautiful.

"He's a cutie, huh? If I wasn't old enough to be his mama, I'd go for it myself."

I look over at the audio lady and realize I've been staring at Blake's image an embarrassingly long time. "Oh, uh, I was just thinking, those monitors should probably be recalibrated. The... color looks a little off to me."

Frank glances up from his repairs. "Color? I hadn't noticed. But have at it if you want to. The more you get your hands on things around here the better."

Sadly, the thing I'm most interested in getting my hands on around here is right in front of my eyes, preparing to go on live TV. I like him. Really, *really* like him. But I decided somewhere between the focus ring and the toggle zoom this morning I'm not going to go out with Blake.

I know I'll have to tell him eventually, but the timing is taken out of my hands when I happen to exit the director's booth at the same time he leaves the studio and we meet in the hallway.

"Cinda," he says with obvious delight.

"Hi," I wheeze, overcome by a rare strain of breath-stealing butterflies. "Nice report on the noon."

"Oh, you saw it? Thanks. So…" He pushes the tips of his fingers into his pockets and rocks back on his heels. "…did you find anything interesting in your office this morning?"

"Uh… yes. The flowers were beautiful. Absolutely… beautiful. Thank you." And now I don't know what to say. He looks so completely adorable up close in person I'm doing a mental speed-rewind of my earlier arguments against dating him. *Why was that a bad idea again?* Oh yes. Logic. Right. It just doesn't make sense.

"You're welcome." Blake gives me a gratified smile. "Glad you liked them. And the card?"

I glance around. "Um, can we go somewhere else to talk?"

We're in the hallway just outside the studio where a steady stream of co-workers passes us in both directions. We might as well be standing in a busy intersection, and I don't necessarily want everyone to overhear us. It could make my remaining couple of weeks here uncomfortable.

"Sure. Want to go downstairs?"

"Yes. Good idea. Frank said he was going to lunch."

Blake follows me down to the engineering office. It's dark and cool as usual. The air smells of roses, and as always, the low murmur of classic Star Trek plays softly in the background.

Blake points at the TV screen in the corner. "I love this episode—I think I must've seen it at least ten times."

Rats. He has no idea how hard he's making this.

His eyes flick away from the TV set and back to my face. He apparently doesn't like what he sees there. "Uh oh. This doesn't look like a yes-I'd-love-to-go-out-with-you face."

I take a breath and launch into the speech I rehearsed in the wee hours of this morning. "It comes down to this. I've got two more weeks here and then, God willing, I'll have a paying position somewhere, and I've still got a whole year of school left. You've got a full-time job, and lots of ambition, and once the young blonde intern is out of sight, I'm sure I'll be out of mind, too. And there are always new interns. And there's just no point in starting anything we have no chance of finishing."

"Wait, wait, hold up. Are you saying you think I asked you out because I've got a thing for interns? Because—"

He has me flustered. I was supposed to give my speech, and he was supposed to listen and then go away, but now we're off on this tangent.

I shake my head. "No. I know there's some... whatever... between us. And we have a few things in common, but that doesn't mean our going out is a good idea."

As if on cue, Mr. Spock's calm steady voice comes from behind me.

"That is... illogical, Captain."

If this conversation weren't so distressing I might have laughed. Blake doesn't look distressed at all. In fact, his frown from a bit earlier has been replaced by a sly, pleased grin.

"So then… you *admit* to feeling… *whatever* for me."

Now I do laugh. "Maybe. A *little* whatever."

"Whatever's good. Whatever's a start."

"But that's my point. We shouldn't start. It just doesn't make sense."

"Do you have a boyfriend?"

Another tangent. I blink. Blink again. "No." My voice sounds defensive.

"But you go out with guys from school."

"Yes." *Where's he going with this?*

"So the other guys you've gone out with—it must have made *sense* for you to date them, but you're not *with* any of them." He takes a step toward me, crowding me with his enticing scent and the heat of his large body. His voice drops low. "Did you feel *whatever* for any of them?"

I retreat a step, causing the back of my thighs to bump into Frank's work table. "I don't think that's any of your business."

He tips his head back, looking down at me through hooded eyes and wearing a sexy grin. "That's a no."

"That's a 'none of your business.'"

Blake moves closer. He leans toward me, forcing me to sit on the edge of the table to preserve the distance between us. And then he angles over me, placing his palms on the table on either side of my hips. I'm not a small woman—medium height and weight— but his big frame surrounding me, the barely controlled power of his body *so close* makes me feel dominated, helpless. And his scent at this close range makes me want to lick my lips.

His gaze goes to my mouth, as if he can read the thought. As if he wants to kiss me. *Oh God.*

I wait, paralyzed by the heat suffusing my body, by the look in his eyes as they meet mine again. My mind is thrashing almost as hard as my heart, trying to decide if I want him to kiss me or not, when he breaks the thick silence.

The powerful inference in his raspy whisper is clear. "You know what you need? *You* need a little more *whatever* in your life."

I swallow and fight for breath. My racing heart is greedily taking all the oxygen away from the rest of me. I try for snarky defiance, but my voice shakes, ruining the effect. "And… I suppose you're just the man for that job…"

Frank's noisy entrance breaks the heavy tension. I jump away from Blake, jostling the work table hard and knocking the soldering iron from its stand. Thankfully, the device isn't on, so no fire alarms will follow our smoldering exchange.

"Oh—Cinda. Blake. Sorry to interrupt." Frank clears his throat and averts his eyes. "I was on my way out the door to lunch when I ran into the GM. I had a very interesting conversation with him that concerns you, young lady. Let me know when you get a minute so we can talk." He starts to back out of the room.

"No. It's fine. Now is good. What's up?"

"Would you like me to leave?" Blake asks, straightening. From the corner of my eye I notice his fists clench in apparent frustration.

I say, "Yes," at the same time Frank says, "Not necessary."

Frank continues, "How'd you like a *job* here at WATV?" His wide smile makes his face resemble a big, friendly Jack o Lantern.

"A job? You mean keep working here through the summer?"

"Yes ma'am, and beyond that, on a part-time basis in the fall if you'd like to."

"Wow. That's… but how…"

"I told the GM a few months ago I'd like to start cutting back, try a sort of semi-retirement thing. But there really wasn't anyone who could replace me who'd be willing to work part-time.

Recently, I told him about you, about how much you've been doing around here, how capable you are. Today he said he'd approve it if I wanted to offer you a salary and see if you'd be interested in a little job-sharing arrangement with me. I could take more time off, and you could work your part-time hours around your classes. What do you say?"

I blink several times, hardly able to believe what I've just heard. "I'd say you've got yourself a part-time engineer."

He laughs and offers me a meaty hand, pumping mine up and down in congratulations. "Great. Great. I thought you'd be pleased. Well, all righty then. I'm half-starved, and Demarc's Barbeque is calling my name with a bullhorn. We'll talk about your salary when I get back. I think you'll be happy with it."

He winks at me and gives my shoulder a pat. Then he turns to Blake. "I see you've found your way down to engineering. We've got reporters who've been at the station ten years and don't know where it is. Wonder how *you* managed to find it so fast?"

Frank punctuates his facetious remark with a hearty laugh and leaves the room, taking with him my last excuse for turning Blake down.

Blake stands facing me, and I'm hyper-aware of the brand new elephant in the room, who is apparently using a whole helluva lot of oxygen, because the space feels tiny and airless suddenly.

"So... looks like you'll be here a bit longer than two weeks, after all."

I take an unsteady breath. "Yes. Looks like it."

"And according to the criteria you laid out earlier, it makes a whole lot more *sense* now for you to go out with me. And now that I will no longer be left at the mercy of that new crop of man-eating interns... I'm going to have to find another way *not* to have any fun."

"Yes. Looks like it," I say again, too unnerved to be original.

"So... what do you say?" He repeats Frank's question.

"I'd say... you've got yourself a date?" *Lord help me.*

CHAPTER EIGHT
FLUTTERS

"He won't tell me where we're going, so how am I supposed to know what to wear?" I'm standing in my closet, looking back over my shoulder at Kenley, who's observing me with a look of outright amazement.

"Where is my sister and what have you done with her?" she says, narrowing her eyes in mock suspicion.

"What are you talking about? *Help me.* He'll be here in forty minutes and I have no idea what to put on."

"This may be the first time in the twenty years I've known you that you've *ever* worried about what you were going to wear. I have *got* to meet this guy."

"No." The word is out of my mouth before I can stop it, and it shocks me—both the strength of my denial and the reason behind it. *I don't want him to meet Kenley.*

As soon as she expressed eagerness to meet Blake, a vision of Tyler's love-sick confession popped into my brain. It shames me. Kenley would never want to take a guy away from me, even if she wasn't in love with Larson.

*But he might want **her**.* God, I thought I was way past this.

I ratchet my tone down a few notches, shrugging. "I mean—I don't know if this is even going to amount to anything, so you shouldn't waste your time meeting him."

Kenley gives me a quizzical look. "Meeting one of your friends is never a waste of time. But Larson does need me there in a half hour, so it won't be tonight. What's the matter? Ashamed of your big sister?"

"No, not at all." Actually the opposite is true. As usual, Kenley looks stunning. She's wearing a strapless royal blue jumpsuit with flowy wide legs, accented by oversized silver hoop earrings and silver arm bangles. She looks like an updated Diane Von Furstenberg model, and any guy's tongue would automatically loll out of his mouth when he saw her. "But I don't want you to be late," I lie.

Larson's parents are in town visiting from New York for a few days, and he's hosting a group of their well-to-do friends from Atlanta's highest social echelon for a cocktail party at his amazing high rise condo. As his fiancée, this is Kenley's first opportunity to play hostess.

I turn the conversation to her evening. "Are you nervous?"

"A little," she admits. "But, all I can do is be myself. If they don't like me, that's too bad. Larson loves me just as I am, and that's all that matters. *You* seem nervous, though."

"I am. A little."

Kenley steps past me into my closet and selects a pair of white jeans then hands them to me. "Well, that's good. It means you actually care. You've always been so blasé about the guys you were going out with, I was starting to get worried."

"Worried about what? That I was a lesbian?" I follow Kenley as she leaves my room and goes to her own closet.

She riffles through the top rack, searching her never-ending wardrobe. "No. That wouldn't worry me. What did bother me was thinking that the messed-up stuff with Momma and Daddy and what happened with Tyler might have…" She looks back over her shoulder at me. "…affected you. That you were never going to let yourself get attached to anyone because you were so turned off to relationships. But I guess you just hadn't met anyone who gave you the flutters yet. And now you have. That's how you know you've found a keeper." She turns around with a big smile and hands me a lime green halter top. "Here. This will look great with your tan."

I shake my head vigorously. "Blake's not a keeper."

"How do you know? That's what I thought at first about Larson."

"We're not a very good match. I just want… we're just going to hang out and have fun."

She quirks an eyebrow at me. "I thought you didn't *do* that. You've always said if it doesn't make sense and isn't going anywhere, then you're not *wasting your time* dating a guy."

"I know. I just… I want to be around him… anyway," I confess, rolling my eyes at my own irrational behavior.

Kenley gives me a satisfied grin and a pert nod. "Right. The flutters. Have fun."

# # #

I go down to meet Blake in the parking lot as planned. He's waiting for me in a new-looking Ford F-150 and gets out when he sees me, coming around to the front of the truck and meeting me on the sidewalk.

"Hi. Wow. You look incredible. Man, the guy behind the seafood counter's going to lose his mind."

"Thank you. Are we going to a seafood restaurant then?" I ask, trying to decipher his strange compliment. "I thought you didn't like it."

He opens the passenger door, and I get in. "No, we're going to the grocery store," he says before closing my door and walking around the front of the truck to the driver's side.

Grocery store?

When he gets behind the wheel, he explains. "I promised you no fun, so I thought we'd go grocery shopping. I'm out of everything, and I need to go anyway, so…"

"Grocery shopping. Okay." I laugh. So he's taking this no-fun thing seriously. "I guess I'm a bit overdressed then."

"Are you kidding? I'm going to be the proudest man at Harry's Market. You're perfect."

As it turns out, Harry's is a blast. I've never seen such an incredible grocery store. The place is out near my parents' former house in Alpharetta, and it is huge. The produce department alone is the size of a normal store.

"And what do you suppose this is?" Blake asks.

We're playing a game called Guess the Exotic Fruit. He's holding up a brown spiky thing.

"A medieval weapon?"

"Errr," he makes a game-show-wrong-answer noise. "I'm sorry. It's actually a durian—treasured for its sweet custard-like flesh."

"Okay, well it still looks painful. Now your turn. Close your eyes." As Blake obeys my command and stands by our cart with his eyes tightly shut, I peruse the display of strange produce and pick one, reading the chalkboard sign above its bin. I've chosen a bright red furry ball covered in yellow quills. He'll never guess it. "Okay ready."

"Hmmm. Let's see... wow. That looks like a tribble, doesn't it? Um... are you sure that's edible?"

"Quit stalling. Take a guess."

"A... rambutan."

My hands come to my hips. "Hey—not fair. You knew that one already. You've been here before, haven't you?"

"Once or twice. Put that tribble in the cart with the medieval mace and let's move on to the stinky cheeses. They have samples of everything, and some of them are so strong, they'll curl your hair."

We spend an hour at the store, sampling foods and filling the cart with exotic foods we've never heard of as well as a few normal staple items. I'm having a marvelous time, and Blake has been smiling almost non-stop, so I think he is, too. I suspect he knew shopping together would actually be fun, after all. In fact... it's already the best date I've ever had.

We're standing in the checkout line when Blake says, "So, for part-two of our no-fun evening, I was thinking we'd go back to my place and cook up some of this stuff. Unless the cheese cubes and edamame hummus samples filled you up."

"Oh. I... uh. I don't know about that." All the lighthearted fun of our evening comes to a screeching halt when I think of going back to Blake's apartment. Here under the bright fluorescent lights and surrounded by refrigerator cases, I've found it hard not to stare at his lips, not to think about that almost-kiss in the engineering dungeon yesterday.

If we go back to his place, I'm afraid of what might happen, of what he might expect. He's a twenty-four year old man, after all. If the nineteen and twenty year olds I've been dating push me for quick sex, then how much more will Blake expect?

And everything's been going so well. I'm afraid sex will just ruin it all. Looking over at him—the tight, athletic body, the beautiful face, the big hands—there's no doubt he's had plenty of opportunity and therefore a lot of experience.

I however, have an extremely limited sexual repertoire. Even if I had vast experience it might not help, because I'm pretty sure I suck at the whole thing. It would take him about… oh ten minutes in bed… and he'd figure that out. And then this *whatever* we have going on will be over. I'm not ready for it to be over yet.

"Can we go out instead?"

"Out." He seems to be thinking. "You mean… to a restaurant?"

Great. Now he thinks I want him to spend a lot of money on me or something. "No. That would qualify as *fun*." I smile to let him know I'm teasing. "Let's just go to a fast-food place. Or get something from a drive-thru and eat it in the car."

He studies my face for a minute. "Stay here with the cart—I'll be right back." And then he dashes away, back through the store. A few minutes later he returns carrying a box containing a rotisserie-roasted chicken, a long, paper-wrapped French bread stick, and a couple of deli cartons. A bottle of wine is tucked under one of his arms and he's dangling a bag of ice from two fingers.

I take the ice and the wine and place them in the cart. "Forget some things?" I ask.

"We're going to have a picnic," he announces.

CHAPTER NINE
PARTY CRASHER

"I hate to tell you this," I say as we climb into his truck. "But a night-picnic sounds like fun, too."

He shakes his head. "Don't worry. It won't be. I just realized I don't have any repellant with me, so the mosquitos are going to have all the fun."

I laugh. "Oh, good. I was getting worried there for a minute."

The Chattahoochie River is only a ten minute drive from Harry's. There's a seven-mile linear park running along its banks, featuring playgrounds, boat ramps, and fishing. And of course picnic areas.

Blake pulls into one of the river walk's parking lots—empty at this hour. He spends a minute arranging the perishable items into one bag with the ice, then grabs the sack containing our food and gets out of the truck. He hands me the bag.

"Hold on to this for a minute. I've got a flashlight in here somewhere. If one of us trips on a tree root and breaks an ankle, we *really* won't have any fun." He rummages through the storage box in the pickup's bed and comes up with a flashlight, handing it to me and taking back the bag. "Okay, let's go."

I turn the light on and lead us to a picnic table near the water's edge. The flashlight is almost unnecessary, as there's a large, nearly full moon out, and it's quite bright in the clearing near the water. A rustle of movement and soft quacking alerts me to the presence of a group of ducks, settled on the riverbank for the night. One of them lifts his head to check us out then folds it back against his wing.

When I was little and picnicked at the river with my family, I was terrified of the ducks. They could be quite aggressive in their quest for breadcrumbs, and one even pecked at my sandal-clad toes. Remembering the long-ago incident, I'm relieved these are hibernating for the night.

Blake begins pulling our dinner supplies from the bag and setting them on the table. I shine the light on the containers to see what he chose.

"Potato salad, black-eyed peas. Yum. I hope there are some forks in there."

"Ta da." He pulls out plastic forks and rests them atop the carton lids. Then he draws the boxed chicken from the bag and produces a stack of napkins. He shoves the bag aside and invites me to sit on the table-top. "I'll be right back. I left the wine in the truck."

I climb onto the tabletop and wait for him, looking out over the dark river. It's so quiet, peaceful. Beautiful actually. The moon reflects off the river, which seems almost still tonight. In moments, Blake is back, holding the wine bottle in one hand and pulling a Swiss army knife out of his pocket with the other.

"Hope Chardonnay is okay with you," he says, prying the cork from the bottle with the corkscrew part of his multi-tool. "I thought it would go well with the chicken."

"Oh, you even thought of the wine-pairing huh?" I laugh. "What about glasses?"

Blake's head drops back and he groans, staring up at the sky for a half-second before giving me an apologetic glance. "No... glasses are reserved for *pre-planned* picnics. At impromptu no-fun picnics like this one, you just drink out of the bottle. You don't have a thing about cooties, do you?"

"If I did, the wine would kill them all, so we're good." I reach for the bottle, and Blake hands it to me. I tip it and take a drink, then give it back to him. "Cheers."

He grins at me and takes a drink from the bottle. "An excellent vintage," he says in an effete wine-snob tone.

He comes to sit beside me on the tabletop, and we dig into the potato salad and black-eyed peas, eating them right from the containers since we don't have plates. Blake rips a chunk from the French bread stick for me and one for himself. Since we have no clean knife for politely dividing the roasted chicken, we use our forks to stab it and pull shreds of succulent meat from the carcass.

"Meat good," Blake grunts in a Neanderthal voice. "Do I know how to show a girl a bad time, or what?"

I giggle, having a ridiculously *good* time. Throughout the strange meal, we pass the wine bottle back and forth. But I can't help noticing the weight of the bottle doesn't seem to change much whenever he takes a turn. He's either taking baby sips or faking it.

Before long I can't eat anymore, and I *certainly* shouldn't drink anymore. My head is buzzing pleasantly. I need to stop now before I cross over into *carry-me-to-the-car-Blakey* territory and resemble Alissa more than I care to.

As I re-wrap the remaining bread, Blake takes our empty food containers to a trashcan and disposes of them then comes back and sits beside me on the table. We're facing the river, both watching its slow, dark flow. The temperature has dropped, and there's a slight breeze now. Noticing my shiver, Blake puts an arm around me and draws me tightly against his warm side. "We should probably head back soon. You have class in the morning, right?"

"Yes." I nod in agreement. But I don't want to go. Grocery shopping and eating like cavemen in the dark has been by far the best time I've had in a long time. That scares me a little. It's not because of what I've been doing, but with whom I've been doing it. If *this* is fun with Blake, anything would be. And even more frightening… I'm desperate for him to kiss me.

The moonlit night, the dark riverside park, the wine warming my veins while his arm around me and his body next to me warm the rest of me—all of it is combining to give me the flutters on a grand scale. I didn't even know being with a guy could feel like this. Just *thinking* about kissing him has me more turned on than doing the actual deed with Tyler ever did.

Blake must be feeling the same pull because when I let my hand rest lightly on his leg, he turns to look at me, and his eyes in the moonlight are intense. His chest is rising and falling more like a guy who's out for a jog than one who's sitting still, barely moving a muscle.

"Cinda…"

"What?" I whisper.

"I don't want to rush things… or scare you. But I have to do this…" He leans in, and places a finger lightly under my chin to tilt it up. I think for sure he's going to kiss me, but he stops.

Please. Do it. "I'm not scared," I prompt him with a lie.

And then he does. From the first moment of contact I'm in absolute pheromone-induced shock. His lips are soft, warm, perfect. What he *does* with them is perfect. And then his tongue pushes past my lips, and my mouth opens to welcome him. As our tongues play and explore, I lift my hands and sink them into the silky curls of his hair. It feels just as good as I knew it would all those times I was dying to touch him.

I draw my hands down his face and over his cheekbones, enjoying the rough texture of his night-beard stubble. The muscles of his jaw flex under my hands as his kiss turns stronger, deeper. Now I'm not content to sit beside him—my insides are restless, energized. I want more contact. I slip my hands around his neck and pull myself against him as tightly as I can in our awkward position. His arm slides around my back, trying to help me get closer.

With a grunt of excitement, Blake leans forward, lowering me back over his arm and levering his body on top of mine on the picnic table. When there's a crunch and crackle behind me, he sweeps the bread bag off the table with gusto, seeming as anxious to feel me underneath him as I am to feel his weight on top of me.

I've got one leg extended, the other bent with my foot resting on the bench, and he settles into the cradle of my body, fitting absolutely perfectly there. Now I can feel all of him, feel his excitement, and it only increases mine. Our kisses grow harder, more intense.

For the first time in my twenty years of life, I'm awash in lust. Maybe my friends who gushed about the wonders of sex weren't making it all up after all. I mean, we're both fully dressed and just kissing, and I'm feeling things that make me want to feel *more* things.

My plan of staying away from his apartment to avoid the issue of sex is failing miserably. Apparently anywhere Blake and I are alone together, sex is going to be an issue. Even outside on top of a concrete picnic table. He's just too attractive, and my reaction to him is too overwhelming.

Suddenly, my body jerks in shock and I pull my mouth away from his with a little scream. "Get off. Get off."

Blake leaps off of me, his face twisted in concern. "What happened? Did I hurt you? Am I too heavy?"

I'm sure he thinks he's bruised my spine by pressing it into the hard table. "No. No, it's not you." I scramble to my feet and stand on the tabletop, shaking all over. "One of those ducks just pecked me."

"What?" he says with a half-laugh.

"Ducks. They hate me. One of them pecked my pinky toe." I glance at his amused grin. He's not taking this seriously. "Really hard." I add.

Now that he's no longer concerned about having harmed me in some way, Blake laughs out loud. "Are you referring to the small feathered creatures, sleeping peacefully right over there?"

I give him a dirty look. "Fine. Laugh. But I'm telling you something pecked my toe, and unless you have a bill tucked away in some strange secret location, it had to have been a duck."

"Well, no, since you've asked, I do *not* have an extra pecker with which I attack the toes of unsuspecting young ladies. But..." He looks around, holding his hands out to the sides. "I don't see the suspect. And I'm detecting some sort of duck phobia here, or maybe a conspiracy theory?"

I frown at his sarcastic tone and bemused expression. "It's here somewhere. He's waiting for me to get down so he can peck me again."

Blake's voice is filled with merriment. "Maybe he was jealous—maybe he wanted a taste—"

A loud quack comes from under the picnic table.

"See? I told you," I hiss in a loud whisper.

He squats down to peer underneath then scrambles back in a hurry as a huge mallard charges him. Blake barely gets to his feet before the duck starts striking his legs.

"What the hell?" he yells, still semi-laughing. He kicks half-heartedly at the duck in self-defense, causing it to retreat.

"Watch out, he's coming back," I squeal, pointing and hopping on my toes.

Sure enough, the mallard is moving in from behind Blake for a sneak-attack.

"Ow—fucking duck." Blake narrowly dodges a second bill-strike to the calf, skipping to the side, putting him further away from my refuge on the table.

"Wait—you can't leave me here," I cry.

"You're safe up there. Don't worry." Blake dodges to the other side as the crazy duck makes another run at him. "You should get to the truck while he's after me."

I look over at Blake's pickup. The parking lot seems miles away. He's right—the picnic is definitely over, and it's time to go. But try as I may, I can't get my feet to move. My legs feel like concrete pillars, and my feet are stapled to the tabletop.

Blake has succeeded in drawing the duck further away, running backward a step or two ahead of the fierce fowl's advance. He takes his eyes off his adversary to motion to me. "Come on—this is your chance."

"I… I don't think I can. I'm… frozen."

He stops in place, looking at me, and the duck catches up with him. "Ow! You little son of a—hold on, Cinda—I'm coming to get you."

I nod silently, watching in terror as the other ducks begin to wake and stir from their resting places. "Hurry," I mewl. Later I will probably be ashamed of my cowardice, but at the moment, I am too afraid to care what a weenie I must look like.

Blake makes his way back to the table, kicking periodically at his miniature attacker, hot on his heels. When he reaches me, he turns around, offering his back. "Get on."

I immediately follow his command, clambering onto his wide back and clinging to his shoulders for dear life. They're huge and hard—well, he said he was a baseball player—he must still work out, unless he was just born this way, which would be all kinds of unfair. I clamp my thighs on his hips, and his large hands come around to grip them firmly.

"Hang on tight," he says and takes off for the truck, laughing and cursing as the manic mallard gives chase and nips at his ankles. Setting me down beside the passenger door of the pickup, Blake shields me while I climb inside.

I slide across the seat and open the driver's side door so he can jump right in when he makes it around. He dives in, bringing a whoosh of night air with him. The slamming of his door cuts off a last long angry quack.

We both sit, breathing loudly for a moment before turning to each other and bursting into laughter.

"What did he want? Is it possible for ducks to have rabies?" I ask between giggles.

"Doubt it. He probably smelled the bread. And I'll bet there's a nest over there near the table somewhere. He's just protecting his woman. Damn serious about it, too." He reaches down and rubs his lower leg.

I flip on the overhead interior light, craning to see his legs in the shadowed cab. "Are you okay? Did he bite you? Maybe we should go to the walk-in clinic in case he did have some disease."

"I'm fine," he insists. "Didn't break the skin. I'm just going to have some strange-shaped bruises on my calves and shins." He shakes his head. "That was the damndest thing."

I sit back against the leather seat. "I told you, ducks hate me. Thank you for carrying me, by the way. I'm sorry I was too much of a baby to run by myself."

"No worries." He gives me a provoking grin. "It was kind of fun to see Miss Spock acting irrational for a change."

"Fine. Keep laughing." I point at his face. "But I'll bet the next time you see a duck, you'll make a wide path around it."

"And I bet the next time I suggest making dinner at my place, you'll consider it. You probably regret saying no now, don't you?" He pauses, studying my frozen expression. "What did you think was going to happen, Cinda? I wasn't planning to lock all the doors and attack you, you know."

No, but I might have attacked you... especially if you had kissed me the way you did a few minutes ago.

"I just... didn't feel comfortable."

And I don't feel much more comfortable now. As the shock and fear of the attack fades, memories of Blake's enticing kisses are coming back. I wasn't nearly ready to stop—one more reason to hate ducks. The fact that he heroically rescued me from my nemesis, well it doesn't *hurt* his appeal.

He starts the truck and pulls it out of the lot, still chuckling to himself, about the duck, I guess. At least I hope he's not laughing at me because I'm too scared to go back to a man's apartment with him.

Trying to change the topic, I say, "So, you certainly seem to know a lot about aquatic bird behavior."

"Oh—I grew up in the country."

"Really? I lived in the suburbs all my life. Where did you grow up?"

"Sparta. Little dink place. Man, I couldn't wait to get out of there."

"So, you were a farm boy then?"

His mouth twists and settles into a grim line. His eyes stay on the road before us. "No. We didn't have a farm. I just lived out in the sticks, on a remote county road."

"Sounds kind of fun," I say, encouraging him to continue talking about himself, but he doesn't take the hint. He just gives a noncommittal shrug. Again I get the impression there's something he's hiding.

He's super-quiet now, and it's starting to feel awkward. I don't like the silence, because it gives me too much time to think about our kiss, his touch, the way the muscles of his shoulders and neck moved powerfully under my hands as he ran with me on his back.

As my mind wanders in that direction, the temperature in the truck cab seems to increase exponentially. Even watching him drive is erotic—the flex of the muscles in his forearms as he moves the steering wheel, the shifting of muscle in his legs as he brakes at traffic lights—it's like some kind of sexy performance-art-on-wheels.

"I like your truck."

That gets him smiling. "Thanks. And Hank thanks you." He pats the dashboard as if it's the head of a faithful pet dog.

"You named your truck?"

"Yep. He's my first new vehicle, and I'm not ashamed to admit I'm a little bit attached."

That gives me pause. He's twenty-four, and this is his first new car? I'm car-less at the moment, but I was given a new car as soon as I turned sixteen. At Momma's insistence, I had a new model about every two years after that, until recently when we all had to turn in our expensive leased vehicles.

"So you bought used before? That's very green of you—re-use, repurpose," I say.

He glances over at me, wearing an expression that tells me he's weighing whether he wants to reveal whatever's on his mind. "There's that... and this is the first job I've had that paid anything really. My first job out of school was in Macon. That's a tiny starter market, and let's just say I was doing well to afford the gas for my old used P-O-S."

"Did that car have a name, too?"

"It did." He gives me a smile so potent it should come with a warning label. "But I don't think I should mention it in front of a lady."

We pull into the parking lot of my apartment complex, and Blake parks his truck in one of the visitor spots near the main sidewalk. He turns off the engine and sits for a second before shifting to face me.

"So... I hope you had a really no-fun time tonight."

"Oh I did. That was one of the most no-fun dates I've ever had, as a matter of fact." I play along, expecting him to return my smile.

Instead his expression is rather uncertain. "Actually, I was hoping it would turn out a *little* better than that. I *can* cook, and I was planning to make you a nice dinner."

I cover his hand with mine. "I had a great time. It would have been perfect, actually, if it hadn't turned into Night of the Living Duck."

Blake looks down at my hand resting on his, gives a slight smile, and flips his hand over, interlacing his fingers with mine. "Good. Because it was feeling pretty perfect to me there for a while, too." He looks up at my face in the dark cab. "You don't think some jealousy-crazed duck is going to come out of nowhere if I try to kiss you again, do you?"

Grinning despite my nervousness, I whisper, "I think we're safe."

Blake uses our joined hands to pull me to him, leaning over to bridge the distance. Our lips meet, and his kiss is different this time, slowly exploring, relaxing me, drugging me.

Then I realize it was just a gateway drug. Now that I'm hooked he's bringing on the fully addictive stuff, longer, wetter kisses that grind and pull and make suggestions I'm all-too-willing to take. *How does he do this to me?* Within a few short minutes, we've gone from sweet-goodnight-kiss to I'd-like-to-swallow-you-whole-and-lick- the-plate-clean hunger.

Both of us are breathing rapidly through our noses, and Blake's hand is caressing from my waist to my ribcage and inching ever higher. I feel like I should slow things down, but my hormones are fighting with my brain cells. *One more minute,* they plead. I have never experienced this sort of pull toward another human being before—everything he does feels amazing, and I can't get close enough. I want to absorb him.

From beside us, the double-beep of a car security system being activated yanks me out of my sex-merized state. I pull back, and Blake lifts his head, staring down the guy who had the audacity to park next to us. At Blake's threatening glare, the guy quickly turns away and walks up the sidewalk toward my building.

"Parking lots these days—they just don't afford the privacy they used to," Blake says. When I laugh softly, he continues, "I hate to say goodnight. Should I come up for a little while?"

And now I'm all the way back in reality. Taking in Blake's tempting kiss-swollen lips and sexy-sleepy green eyes, I'm desperately tempted to say 'yes'. I don't want to say goodnight either.

But the distinct possibility of sex ruining things is still there. More importantly, Kenley could be up there, and as much as Blake seems to like me, I still don't want him to meet her. Not yet. I mean, if he finds *me* attractive, I dread the day he gets a look at my sister. She's the A choice and I'm the alternate. She's the solid object, and I'm the shadow that always follows it.

When Blake sees us standing side-by-side, whatever beauty I may possess will suddenly seem like a pale reflection of Kenley's. I don't want to see that "diminishing" effect happen in his eyes. I'm enjoying being the main attraction for once, and I'm not ready for that to end.

"I don't think that's a good idea," I say, settling back into my seat and readjusting my clothes.

Blake nods, immediately accepting my decision. "Right. You're absolutely right. Too fast." He grabs my hand and squeezes it. "You're just so beautiful and sexy—you make me want things I have no right to want yet."

Yet. So he wants to keep seeing me. In confirmation of my thoughts he says, "I'd like to take you out again. If you want to. Maybe next time we could do something that's actually fun."

He's already got me so entranced I'm a little afraid to see what he'll come up with when he's *trying* to dazzle me. "Okay," I say anyway.

Blake's answering smile is luminous in the dark truck cab. "Great. Tomorrow night?"

"Oh… I really can't. I have to study the next couple of nights. I have a Circuits and Electronics test on Friday morning."

"Friday night then? We can celebrate your kicking ass on your test."

"Okay. Friday night." I give him a quick peck and slide out of the cab.

At the end of the sidewalk, just before stepping onto the stairs, I look back. Blake is still there in his truck. He lifts a hand and gives me a sweet smile that fries every circuit I have. *Oh my.*

The breath leaves my lungs all at once, and my heart flips in a thrilling sensation that logic has no hope of competing against.

CHAPTER TEN
FRIDAY NIGHT HORROR SHOW

"Why is he picking you up at eleven o'clock at night? This isn't a booty call, is it?" Kenley's face contracts in a worried frown. I've asked her to help me do some light makeup for my date tonight, and we're sitting in her bathroom, facing each other.

As soon as she lifts the mascara wand from my lashes I shake my head. "No. He says there's something special he wants me to see."

Her lips purse, and her blonde brows pull together. She reaches into her enormous cosmetics case and retrieves a thin brush and a pot of lip gloss. "Well, if it turns out to be the inside of his bedroom, I want you to walk right out of there. He should have more respect for you than that."

"Says the Queen of the Booty Call," I tease.

Once again, Kenley's planning to spend the night at Larson's. She holds up her left hand displaying the rock I couldn't have missed even if she'd been a half mile away. In a fog bank. At night.

"Hey, *he's* already put a ring on it. It's different. And if it weren't for the mandatory society wedding with a cast of thousands, we'd be married already. Larson's more eager for the wedding day than I am. This Blake guy—we don't know his intentions. Not yet. In fact, I really think I should meet him this time, maybe get a photocopy of his license, before he takes you out on a midnight mystery date."

"No, Kenley." My tone is harsher than I intended, but this thing with Blake is so new, I really want to keep it to myself for now. "I'm not a fifteen year old going out on her first date, and I don't need you to give him your stamp of approval. You're starting to sound like Momma."

Her face instantly contorts into a mask of horror. "Wow. I don't think you've ever said something so mean to me before."

I'm overcome with guilt. It *was* a mean thing to say, and what's more, it was motivated not by anything she's done, but by my own insecurity. It hasn't been easy to be the younger sister of someone who's automatically the prettiest girl in any room, but Kenley doesn't deserve snarky remarks from me. She *is* unreasonably beautiful, but she's also my best friend and she's been my greatest ally against Momma's craziness all these years. Without her, I don't know what I would have done.

"I'm sorry. I think I'm just tense. But I shouldn't be taking it out on you. Forgive me?"

She wraps her arms around me. "Of course. And I *was* being pushy and nosy. Please do tell me if I ever get like Momma so I can jump off the nearest bridge. I'll meet your Blake when and if you're ready."

I smile at her. "Thanks. And thanks for the makeup. How do I look?"

She leans back, surveying her handiwork. "Like a million bucks."

"Well, you should know... Mrs. Overstreet."

She sticks her tongue out at me and then beams as I leave the bathroom. At a couple minutes till eleven I go downstairs to meet

Blake in the parking lot. This time I climb into his truck cab before he even has the chance to get out and open the door for me.

"Hi."

"Hi." He leans over for a quick peck then back again to check out my look. "You're stunning."

My face heats with pleasure. "Thank you. You look nice, too."

He does. Although *nice* is a pitiful understatement. He's wearing plaid shorts and a well-fitted expensive-looking t-shirt. The muscles that felt so good to me a few nights ago are more apparent now than they've been in his work clothes. I get a powerful mental picture of him pulling up the bottom of that t-shirt and lifting it over his head, and suddenly I'm possessed with the desire to see him shirtless again.

When I first got in the truck and Blake kissed my cheek, I got a whiff of his incredible cologne and of soap, but now all I can smell is... baking bread? He must have had a little snack on the drive over—it *is* late, a long time since supper. I know from being around Larson that big guys like him and Blake eat often.

"So, are you going to tell me where we're going now?"

"Not yet." He grins, keeping his eyes on the road.

"If your plan is to do some kind of spooky graveyard tour or something, I have to tell you... *that* would be legitimately no-fun for me."

"Oh, afraid of ducks *and* ghosts, huh? The list of irrational fears grows."

I slap lightly at his arm. "No. I don't even believe in ghosts. That's why it wouldn't be any fun."

"Okay, well, no worries, because that was *not* my plan for this evening. And don't even try to guess what it is, because you will *fail*."

The challenge in his tone eggs me on. "Ooh. Throwing down the gauntlet. Let's see… what do I get if I guess it right?"

He narrows his eyes in contemplation. "Hmm… you get to pick the next date. Anything you want."

That sets my nerves simmering. He already wants a third date? We've just begun the second one. "Okay… that sounds like a good deal."

Before I can make my first guess, Blake lifts a hand from the wheel, extending his pointer finger. "But—to make it fair, if you fail to correctly guess in three tries, then *I* get a prize."

I narrow my eyes at him, suspicious. "What kind of prize?"

"I get to walk you upstairs to your apartment at the end of the night. We're not going to get home until at least three a.m., so I should do that anyway, just for safety's sake."

Knowing Kenley will be at Larson's, I feel a little safer agreeing. A *little* safer.

"All right. You're on. But under those terms, I'm going to need a hint."

Blake glances over at me, smiling. "Okay then—it's somewhere in Atlanta."

"What a sucky hint. You can't cheat your way up to my apartment, you know. You have to do better than that."

He laughs. "Can't blame a guy for trying. All right. Reach into the back seat and get that bag. Geez, I might as well forfeit now."

I turn in my seat and see the bag. Reaching back, I grab it and bring it forward onto my lap. When I open it, I suddenly understand the baking bread smell. The bag is filled with… toast. There are a couple of squirt guns and a roll of toilet paper as well.

I glance up at him, baffled by the bag's bizzare contents, and shake my head. "I got nothin'," I confess.

"Seriously?" He laughs. "I thought you'd figure it out right away. So that means you're a virgin, then."

My eyes blink rapidly, my heart rate suddenly going nuts. How did a bagful of bread, water toys, and bathroom tissue give him that impression? And are we really going to talk about our respective sexual histories right here and now? I haven't even had a drink yet, for Pete's sake.

Blake laughs louder. "You should see your face right now. I'm not talking about *that* kind of virginity. Have you ever heard of the Rocky Horror Picture Show?"

I shake my head.

"Oh, well this is gonna be awesome then. It's a movie. But it's more like an experience. They've been showing it since 1975, and people are crazy over it. Some of them have gone hundreds of times, and they dress up like the characters—well, you'll see. They call people who've never been to it 'virgins' and try to embarrass them. Just play along and don't admit it when we get inside. And follow my lead when it comes to the toast and water."

"Okay…" I say a bit hesitantly. I don't quite get the idea of going to an old movie where people dress up and bring props—it sort of sounds like a legitimate no-fun date to me, honestly.

By the end of the night, I am a convert. The movie itself is totally cheesy, but it's obviously supposed to be, and it was hilarious fun to watch the die-hard cos-players act out the entire film at the front of the theater, dressed in perfect replicas of the wild on-screen costumes. Blake clued me in when it was almost time to throw the toast at other movie-goers, and I was glad we were armed with the water pistols when the rainstorm scene occurred and other people started splashing and shooting us.

We leave the theater damp, tired, and thoroughly entertained. When we reach the sidewalk just outside, I hear a guy's voice call out Blake's name.

He takes my arm and starts leading me briskly toward the parking lot, as if he hasn't heard it.

"Blake. Blake Branham."

Now I know he's heard the man, but he doesn't stop or turn around. I guess he doesn't feel like chatting with any news-fans tonight. Seems a bit rude to ignore the guy, but what do I know? I've never been on-air and had people recognize me out in public. I keep walking with him and wait as he unlocks his truck and opens the door for me.

"Blake—hey man—I was calling you. I guess you didn't hear me." I turn around to see the fan, obviously undeterred by Blake's non-response, has chased us across the parking lot and is now standing at his side wearing a huge smile.

Blake pretends surprise. "Oh—Ronnie. No, I didn't hear you. Wow—it's been a long time—great to see you."

Okay. So *not* a fan. They're old friends. I'm instantly curious about this guy who's known Blake so much longer than I have.

"Yeah, I moved here about a year ago. What're you doing in Atlanta?" Ronnie asks.

"I took a job with a local TV station. I'm a news reporter now."

The guy nods, obviously impressed. "Nice. Must make some pretty good coin for that. Far cry from the old—"

Blake interrupts him. "Ronnie, this is Cinda. Cinda, this is Ronnie, a friend of mine from the... neighborhood back in Sparta."

"So nice to meet you," I say, extending a hand, which he takes with a smile and a nod.

We all chat a couple of minutes about the movie, but I can sense Blake's restlessness to end the conversation and leave. He's shifting his stance and darting his eyes at the truck. Maybe they weren't exactly friends, then. I don't know. Whatever's going on, there's some sort of weird dynamic, and Blake is definitely acting strangely.

"So we should hang out sometime—us Sparta guys have to stick together, you know? I'm here with a couple of guys tonight, but I want you to meet my wife, Shaunda. We could have a double-date or something," Ronnie suggests, and he seems sincere.

"Sounds good. I'm really busy, and I never know my work schedule too far in advance, but we'll do that sometime. Give me a call at the station. It's WATV."

Ronnie gives Blake a quizzical look, as if he's picking up on the strange vibe as well now. "Okay then. Well, good to meet you, Cinda. Y'all have a good night."

Once inside the quiet of his truck, I wonder if Blake will address what just happened, if he'll explain his hurry to get away from his old hometown friend. But he doesn't mention it. He just asks what I thought of my "virgin" experience at Rocky Horror.

"I thought it was fantastic. And weird. But mostly fantastic. So… were you and Ronnie good friends?"

He shakes his head dismissively, his bottom lip protruding in a little frown as he starts the ignition and pulls out of our parking spot. "Neighborhood buddies, when we were kids. I haven't talked to him in a long time."

"So… you don't go back to Sparta much then?"

Still without looking at me, he shakes his head again, keeping his eyes on the road ahead. "Hardly ever." He worries his lip with his top teeth then lets it go. "There's… not much there." And that's all he says. His tone does not invite further questions.

I know his mom still lives in Sparta—he told me that earlier, so the statement strikes me as strange. He's never mentioned his father. If anyone understands parental issues, I do. But even I visit my parents on a fairly regular basis. Maybe guys are different. I remember Mitzy, the mother of Kenley's ex-fiancé, talking about how she dreaded "losing" her son when they got married because that's what happened when boys left home.

"Oh—this is a great song." Blake hits the button to turn the radio up almost uncomfortably loud. He might as well be wearing a neon sign that reads, "I don't want to talk about it."

I get the message, and I don't push the subject. But it does worry me. Once again, he's being evasive, and I get the feeling he's hiding things about himself, about his past. The emotional closeness I've been feeling with him tonight has taken a hit. At the same time, I find myself craving a different kind of closeness more than ever.

I glance over at Blake, the wetness that's darkened and curled his hair making him somehow even more appealing. Heat pulses in my stomach like the flashing yellow caution light we're driving under. I *want* him to walk me upstairs. I want a goodnight kiss. But how much more do I want?

Part of me immediately volunteers an answer—*everything*. Another part further north is still terrified to enter sex into this equation. Just observing Blake's easy, athletic way of walking and moving the past few days, remembering the skill and wow-factor of his kisses, it's clear he's some kind of sex aficionado. The boy drips been-there-done-that.

And instead of growing more relaxed about the whole thing, I'm now even more stressed about my own lack of skills and my previous less-than-stellar sexual experiences. It's entirely possible the reason sex was so unpleasant before is… that I am *bad* at it.

When Blake finds out I'm some sort of sexual imbecile or a cold fish, his interest in me will evaporate.

And as Kenley so astutely observed before my first date with him, I *care* about this one. I'm starting to care more and more in fact, and I enjoy spending time with Blake too much to let it end now. Of course, if I keep putting him off and pushing him away physically, it might end for another reason.

"Hey."

Blake's voice gets my attention. I realize I've been riding in silence, twisting my fingers together in my lap the way my troubled thoughts are twisting through my brain. I look over at him.

"If you don't want to invite me in, that's totally okay, you know," he says, referring to our wager from earlier. He gives me a sweet smile. "I mean—I gave you the answer before you had a chance to make your three guesses, so our deal's null and void. And it's not like we've got a deadline here. I've rushed into enough things in my lifetime that I've learned when it's worth it to wait."

My body instantly relaxes. "I wasn't worried about that."

Blake's teeth gleam whitely in the dark cab. "Liar," he whispers. "Why don't you just talk to me, Cinda? Tell me what you're thinking."

Can I? Can I just admit my fears and get them out into the open? Will that help or will it just hasten the end of whatever's going on between us?

No. I can't. I suck at talking about feelings and stuff like that. Even if I did feel comfortable enough with Blake to tell him everything, I'd probably say it all wrong and make things ten times worse. And here I was getting annoyed with *him* for being secretive.

I shake my head and say in a tight voice. "It's nothing."

Blake sighs. "Okay." He doesn't like that answer.

For the first time in my life, I'm truly jealous of my sister. Kenley has always known how to talk to guys, how to attract them. We don't discuss stuff like this, but she probably also knows what to do when she gets alone with one. I mean, they certainly kept coming back for more. Even before Larson, everyone she dated seemed to think she was *the one.*

I've never been anyone's *one.* In fact, for all I know, Blake is dating lots of people. Maybe he went out with someone last night and another girl the night before that when I stayed in to study. Maybe that's why he's less-than-forthcoming about his life. *Maybe he has a girlfriend.*

"What did you do last night?" I blurt out the question.

"I went out with a friend," he says, clearly wondering which random field of questions I picked that one from. "Why?"

I *knew* it. My veins are instantly mired with acidic jealously of this unnamed woman. She's probably sophisticated and beautiful, maybe one of the gorgeous female reporters from the station. Maybe someone from his past—maybe Ronnie knows her and *that's* why Blake was in such a hurry to get me away from him.

Oh my God. I laugh to myself. What I want to do is slap myself. My thoughts are becoming completely irrational. Of *course* Blake goes out with other girls, and he should. He's a young, single guy, and we've only gone out *two* times. *What is he doing to me?* I don't even recognize myself. I'm being illogical.

My phone beeps its text message alert, saving me from having to respond. "Excuse me," I say, and pull the phone from my purse. It's Troy.

Troy: Hi. Haven't seen much of you lately. Free tomorrow night?

Me: Yes. Rock climbing?

Troy: Great. Pick you up at 6?

Me. Great. C u then.

I turn off my phone and find I'm breathing easier. The brief exchange with my friend reassures me. And making plans with him was definitely the right thing to do. Blake spends time with other girls—I shouldn't stop seeing other guys just because he's so much more... *more*. It makes sense to keep seeing Troy. Just thinking of his non-demanding, comfortable personality makes my head feel clearer. When this thing with Blake ends, as I know it will, Troy (or someone like him) will be there, waiting for me to get back on track and start making sensible choices again.

We pull up in front of my building at three-thirty a.m. The complex is still and dark. Blake turns the key, and his truck goes still and quiet as well. He reaches for my hand on the seat between us. I let him take it, but I don't look at him.

"Did I do something wrong? You're really quiet."

Now I look over at him, and the worry in his eyes makes me feel awful. "No. I'm sorry. It's me. I was just thinking. Sometimes I get a little too wrapped up in my own thoughts, and I'm probably not very good company."

"No. You are. I had a great time with you tonight."

"Me, too," I respond honestly.

He hesitates before speaking again. "Well, I'm going to insist on walking you up—it's not safe for you to go alone."

"That's fine—you can walk me up. I want you to."

Some of the tension eases from Blake's body, and he gives me a tentative smile. "Okay. Wait right there."

He gets out of the truck and comes around to my door, opening it for me and offering his hand to help me down from the raised cab. We walk up the sidewalk and climb the stairs in silence. I lead Blake to my apartment door. When we reach it, he finally speaks.

"Can I—would you let me hold you a minute before you go in?"

"You want a... hug? Uh, okay." That was not what I was prepared for. I step into his arms, and they go around me.

This is *not* a hug. Hugs are for toddlers and teddy bears and sisters. The solid warmth of Blake's body is amazing, equal parts comforting and exhilarating. He holds me against him, stroking the back of my hair and down my spine again and again. It's not exactly a sensual touch, but it's working for me anyway. Just as it always does around him, my body sparks to life, little fires igniting all over me.

After a few minutes, I lift my head from his chest, any thoughts of Troy and Ronnie long gone, no longer caring about logic and rationality. I want Blake's mouth on mine.

But he must think I'm trying to get away from him. He releases me, and asks, "Would you tell me—I want to know... what you were thinking about in the car. Something bad? About me?" He looks like he's bracing for a damaging response.

"No," I assure him, though I don't really know why he seems so worried. I was thinking about how unreasonably attractive he is and whether I can let myself respond to him the way I want to.

"Something good?" His tone is so hopeful it makes me think of a cute little boy asking for candy in the check-out line at the supermarket.

"Maybe," I tease with a smile, and he smiles back.

"Good. Because all *I've* been able to think about all night is how much I want to kiss you again. I was beginning to worry I'd never get another chance."

Finally giving in to what I want as well, I step toward him, lift my face to his, and whisper, "Here's your chance."

Blake takes my face between his hands, his long fingers reaching almost all the way around my head as he maneuvers his lips over mine. Unlike our last date when he kissed me in his truck, he seems to feel the need for caution tonight. His kiss is gentle, uncertain, not pressing, not pushing. Not enough.

I wrap my arms around his neck and pull myself tightly against him, my own kiss turning insistent. And it must be exactly what he was waiting for. His lungs heave with a harsh exhale, and a low moan comes from his throat as he releases my head and uses his hands to draw me securely against him. Kissing me deeply, he slides one arm firmly around my waist. His other hand moves lower, cupping my hip to align our bodies perfectly, bringing my softest places in line with the hardness of his body.

And I'm in uncharted territory. I've never felt desire like this before. My excitement is turning into the sort of insanity that leads to foolish decisions and *what-the-hell?* flaunting of all possible consequences.

But there *are* consequences. I have to rein this in before it's too late.

I pull my lips away from Blake's. He takes the opportunity to push my hair off my shoulder and shift his hot mouth to my neck. Which is now trembling in ecstasy and joining the *goforitgoforitgoforit* chant that's humming through the rest of my body.

He moves up my neck and whispers against my ear. "Should I come in?"

Yes, yes, oh yes, all my hormones scream in a hallelujah chorus. "No," I say with difficulty, sliding my hands to his chest and putting the slightest barrier between us. "Not tonight."

Blake stares into my eyes. His lips come together in a tight expression that's not hard to read. The sexual frustration is flowing from his pores and surrounding us both in a hazy cloud, but his tone is measured and patient.

"Is there something you're not telling me? Like… maybe you *do* have a boyfriend?"

I shake my head. "No. No—I told you I didn't, and I don't lie."

His voice lowers further, becoming a gentle whisper. "Are you by any chance an *actual* virgin, because if you are, I understand—"

"Blake—no—I'm not. It's not that." I pull away further.

"You're not a hoarder are you?" His tone lightens. I can see in his eyes he's decided not to push it. "Maybe you're worried I'll step through the door and see your piles of magazines stacked to the ceiling, meet your twenty-five cats, and run away screaming?"

Now I laugh. The tension between us is dissipating, and it's becoming easier to think. "I'm allergic to cats."

"Ah—good to know. I'll have to hide my twenty-five cats when you come over to my place then. And you *can* come to *my* place anytime. 152 Peachtree Lane, Unit 2. In fact, come over tomorrow night, and I'll make you dinner. I'll even provide a full complement of utensils for your dining pleasure this time. And actual glasses for the wine."

"Ooh, fancy. I can't tomorrow night, though. I have… plans."

His face falls, reassembling in the mask of concern from a few minutes ago. "A date?"

"Well… yeah."

The concern morphs into displeasure. "Oh. Well… I have to work on Sunday, but maybe I can drop by here earlier tomorrow? Maybe pick you up for lunch, or bring you some if you have to study?"

The innocent suggestion fills me with instant panic. I don't know what time Kenley's planning to come home, if at all. I don't want to chance them running into each other. And now that he knows my apartment number, the danger of that is more real. *Why did I let him walk me up here?*

"I don't think so. I'll be pretty busy during the day."

"Don't tell me you have a lunch date, too? Though I guess I shouldn't be surprised." The look of displeasure has become an outright frown. He's pouting. *How cute.*

I giggle in spite of myself. His perception of me as some kind of hot commodity never fails to tickle me. And also, I want to lighten the mood. I don't want him to think I'm blowing him off.

Besides, although I'm convinced he's hiding things from me, I've just realized I don't have any room to judge him. I'm hiding things, too.

I stand on tiptoe to kiss his tight lips, which soften instantly against mine. When I draw back, I leave my palms on his chest, then slide them slowly down to his abs, which are tightly contracted and moving in and out with his rapid breathing.

"No lunch date. I *do* have to study all weekend. This double-e-major isn't going to kick its own ass. Which means no drop-ins from hot guys, no matter *how* much I might enjoy that."

He seems a bit encouraged, one side of his mouth curling up at my last remark and flirty tone. "You think I'm hot, huh?"

I raise one eyebrow in my best Spock expression.

"Well…" He steps back and his hands fall to his sides. "I guess I'll see you Monday at work then. I'd say I hope you have fun tomorrow night, but that would be a lie." He flashes a rascally grin so adorable I want to open my door and yank him over the threshold.

"I don't want you to lie. I always like the truth better."

I'm surprised to see his grin drop. He lifts a hand, taking two more steps backward. "See you Monday, Cinda." And he turns to go.

I watch him walk to the stairs and disappear from view, wondering why he looked so doubtful.

CHAPTER ELEVEN
DROP-IN

I'm hanging from an artificial rock wall by two fingers and a toe, a guy's hand is planted firmly on my ass, and I feel nothing.

Well, my fingers are killing me, but the ass part? Nada. And that's because the hand belongs to Troy. I have zero doubt that if I'd gone rock-climbing with Blake tonight, and *he* were the one giving me an *assist,* I'd feel quite different about the experience.

"I'm fine. I've got it," I call over my shoulder.

The hand is removed, and from somewhere below me and to the right, Troy says, "Sorry."

He's been super-sweet all evening as usual, but aside from the physical exertion, I'm not enjoying myself the way I usually do with him. His mild personality and laid-back conversation, which I normally find so relaxing, tonight seem... boring. I find myself wishing he'd crack a risqué joke, give me a wicked smile, or suggest some preposterous activity to do that would turn out to be unexpectedly fun.

I reach the top of the wall, ring the bell, and slide down the rope, passing Troy, who's still on his way up. It's not his fault. He's exactly who he's always been. It's me who's changed. And honestly, even if Troy suddenly became the world's wittiest conversationalist,

I probably wouldn't notice—my mind's been somewhere else all night.

As if to underline this fact, I catch only the tail-end of his sentence and realize he's standing beside me at the bottom of the climbing wall. He's unhooking his harness and looking at me, clearly awaiting an answer.

"What'd you say?"

"I said… there are a couple walls we didn't get to, but it's almost nine. We should probably settle our tabs and head out. I like to get a full night's sleep on Saturdays so I can get up and study on Sunday. I know you do, too. I've got an exam Tuesday in Engineering Econ."

"Right. I've got one Wednesday." I nod at him, forcing a smile. *How sensible.* One thing's for sure. If I keep seeing Troy, my GPA will certainly benefit.

The flutters though? They will never happen. Not with him. If Blake was right and what I need is a little more *whatever* in my life, there's only one place I know of to get it.

I excuse myself to go to the ladies' room and do a quick search on my phone for 152 Peachtree Lane… just out of curiosity. As it turns out, Blake's place is about a mile away, between the rock climbing gym and my apartment. Darkness is just falling, and our weekend weatherman warned of potential rain—if he's *not* there, I could be in for a long, dark, and possibly wet jog home. The whole idea is crazy, really.

When I emerge from the restroom, Troy's standing near the check-in desk, shoving his wallet back into his pocket and waiting for me to pay for my climbing session before he drives me home. I settle up, and we step outside together into the sticky evening air.

"So that was fun. We should come back here again," he says.

I give him a non-committal, "Sure," and glance up at the darkening clouds overhead. Yep. Definitely going to rain. I should forget this whole insane idea and just call Blake tomorrow.

"You know what? Why don't you just go on ahead? I think I'm gonna run home," I say.

Troy's eyebrows shoot up. "Run?"

"Yeah. It's not that far, and I need to stop by a friend's house before I go home anyway. I left something there that I need."

"I don't mind driving you."

"No—no. I need to get my miles in this weekend, anyway, and I don't want to trouble you."

He hesitates, giving me the you're-crazy look. "Okay, but I could just wait in the car while you run in and grab it. I don't mind. Besides, it looks like it's about to pour."

"If it does, I'm sure my friend will give me a ride home." *And if I actually find the guts to grab that* something *I need, I may not be going home tonight at all.*

"Well… all right. I guess. So…"

I lean in for an awkward hug. "It was fun. I'll see you in class."

As I'm turning to go, Troy places a hand on my forearm. "Cinda?"

"Hmm?" I turn back to him.

"Can I… would it be okay if I…" He inclines toward me in an obvious here-comes-the-kiss approach.

We never did kiss after our movie date last week. The moment just never felt quite right for me to make a move, and Troy didn't make one either. Of course he would decide to up his game *tonight*. When he's *not* the one I want to kiss.

I lean back, putting on a smile to soften my words. "Troy. I had a nice time tonight. I always have a nice time with you. But…"

He sighs and his shoulders drop. "Your friend... it's a guy, huh?"

Feeling about an inch tall, I answer him honestly. He's a nice person, and he deserves that. "It is."

He nods. "Yeah, I figured. Okay, well. I guess I'll see you in class."

"Right. See you then. Goodnight."

I barely break a sweat by the time I arrive on Blake's quiet street. His place is a lovely brick-covered duplex surrounded by mature trees and mostly single-family homes. One side of his building sits in darkness while warm lamplight shows through the front window of the other. *And I can't remember which side is his.* Great.

I almost decide to keep running. What if he's not even home? What if he is and he's not alone? *This is stupid.* I've never even come close to doing anything like this.

But I really want to see him. He did invite me over for tonight. He'll be happy to see me, right? Before I can think about it too much I step onto his front walk and brace myself for the consequences of my completely illogical decision. Who *is* this girl who leaves a date with one guy to see another, who drops in unannounced to visit a twenty-four-year-old single man at night? I hardly know her, but I do know I feel more alive than I have since I can remember.

Standing on the front step, my gaze goes from one stately front door to the other. He could be doing anything behind that door—cooking dinner for another girl, sleeping... showering. It's the mental picture of a wet, naked Blake that impels me to lift my hand to the doorbell.

Because I don't know which belongs to him, I ring the bell of the duplex side with the lights on. Hopefully it doesn't belong to some young family with infant twins they just put to bed. I hear someone approaching the door, the sound of the deadbolt turning. It opens.

And there stands a beautiful woman.

She's not one of the reporters from the station, but someone should put her on camera somewhere. Long, chestnut hair, perfect pale skin—she's simply stunning, and I'm willing to bet the delicious dinner I smell through the open doorway is being prepared in her honor. By the guy I came here to see.

"Hi," Perfect Girl says with a friendly smile.

"Hi. I'm sorry. I thought my friend lived here, but…" I back away, ready to hit the road for the long jog home. At least I wore running shoes for my date. It's only nine miles or so. In the dark. No problem.

A crack of thunder splits the night and makes me jump. *Beautiful.* A long jog in a thunderstorm. It's about what I deserve for this monumental act of idiocy.

"Do you mean Blake?" the girl says. "This is his place. Blake, honey, there's someone here to see you." She cranes her neck and peers back into the duplex.

Honey. Great. Perfect Girl is not just his dinner date. He *does* have a girlfriend.

I back away further, preparing myself to turn and sprint if necessary to keep from facing him in this uber-awkward situation. And the sky opens up as if someone pulled the zipper on a giant bag of water overhead.

I reach up to wipe a fat drop from my nose. "Oh no. I don't want to disturb your dinner. I was just in the neighborhood—running—going for a little run, and I—"

Blake appears over PG's shoulder. "Cinda?"

Now Perfect Girl whips her head back in my direction. "This is her?" she says, and Blake pokes her side. Her lips roll inward, as if she's trying to hold in words.

He moves past her and steps out onto the front walk. He's wearing a dark t-shirt, and the raindrops are quickly making a splotched pattern on it. He studies me, taking in my wet hair, my athletic wear and shoes. "Cinda—I can't believe you're here. I thought you had a date tonight."

It's a wonder I can respond without stammering. "Yes. I do—did. But it's done. And I thought... but of course *you* have a date, and I'm just going to... finish my run now." I turn away and start to sprint toward the street. *God, what was I thinking?*

I feel Blake's strong fingers clamp on my shoulder. He pulls me around to face him. "Hey—wait. Stop. Where are you going? It's pouring. Come inside."

"No thanks. I really have to go."

"What are you talking about, crazy girl? You just got here. I've been telling Whitney how brilliant you are, and now here you are running at night in a storm." His hand slides down my shoulder and arm to clasp my cold fingers. "Don't make a liar out of me—come on. You're just in time to eat."

Whitney? Is that the woman who answered the door? And he told her about me? I let Blake tug me inside. I'm trembling, either from nerves or my drenched hair and clothing. Probably both.

The inside of his home is warm, in more ways than one. Yes, the temperature feels good on my chilled skin, but the décor is homey. Definitely not bachelor-esque. A large brown leather sectional anchors the living room. Two overstuffed chairs flank a nice stone fireplace.

With its earthy tones and substantial furniture, the place feels masculine, but there are nice comfortable touches, like pillar candles on the mantle, a soft-looking oatmeal-colored throw over one chair arm, and pretty drapes that coordinate with the throw pillows on the sofa and chairs. It looks like a couple lives here.

"Your place is really nice."

Blake smiles down at me as he leads me into the kitchen. "You like it? I'll tell my sister. She picked out everything for me. Hey Whit—you've got another fan. Whitney's a decorator," he explains, nodding toward the gorgeous woman now stirring whatever's on the stove as we enter the room.

Sister. I can't stop a huge smile from emerging.

She reaches across the counter. "Cinda, I'm so happy to meet you. Blake's told me a lot about you." Her tone hints that whatever Blake told her, she approves.

I take her hand. "It's nice to meet you, too." I don't say that Blake's told me nothing about her or any other member of his family. Does he have more siblings? Does Whitney live here with him? If so, the evening's going to turn out a lot differently than I hoped.

"I hope this stuff's not burned," she says to Blake. "He's the chef in the family, not me. I can't even cook crackers and peanut butter."

"But you don't have to cook crack—" I stop and laugh as I get her joke.

"Ugh—crackers and peanut butter. Don't remind me," Blake says, and Whitney snickers.

Seeing my obvious confusion, she begins to explain, "When Blake and I were growing up, our mom—"

"Whitney."

In response to his censoring tone, she edits her tale, turning it into a short story. "We just ate a lot of peanut butter. That's all."

She gives him a wide-eyed what's-your-problem look. He meets it with a quick head shake. Clearly there's something he doesn't want me to know about their past or their mom. I don't know—it's strange. A twinge of foreboding twists in my gut. I hate secrets, and this guy seems to have lots of them.

He relieves her of stove-duty, stirring the dish. "Hope you like Italian. It's Chicken Saltimbocca."

"I've never had that before, but it smells great."

"We have a salad too. Wait—you probably already ate, didn't you?"

"No. I mean yes—but it was a while ago—and my date was pretty strenuous. I worked up an appetite."

Blake's eyes widen then narrow, and a line forms between his brows, but he says nothing, just turns back to the stove and adds some chopped fresh herbs to the dish he's cooking.

Even if supper hadn't been three hours ago, I'd still want a bite of this. The food smells nearly as appetizing as Blake looks, and that's saying a lot. Now that I have a chance to observe him through un-panicked eyes, I'm realizing he's not dressed for a dinner date.

His dark t-shirt is paired with black track pants, loose through the thighs and calves, though they do hug his hips and bottom quite nicely. His feet are bare and... really nice. I've never really liked feet, but his are cute, in a big, size thirteen kind of way, lightly tanned with white square nails.

He glances up and notices me looking him over then glances down at himself. "Yeah, I'm pretty wet I guess. So are you. I'm gonna change." He turns off the heat and slides the pan to the side, away from the hot eye. "I'll get you something to put on, too. All my stuff will be huge on you, but at least it'll be dry."

"I'm sorry I don't have any extra clothes with me," says Whitney. *Okay, so she doesn't live here.*

"No, I'm fine in this." My wet t-shirt is plastered to me, revealing the dark sports bra underneath. My black skort isn't transparent, but it's pretty drenched as well. A shiver goes through my body, revealing my lie.

Blake shakes his head, coming around the counter and looking me up and down. "At least let me throw your shirt in the dryer. It'll be ready by the time dinner's finished."

"I'll help her," Whitney volunteers and hops off the bar stool. "Come with me, Cinda."

She leads me down the hallway to what I assume is Blake's bedroom. Glancing up from the dresser drawer she's rummaging through, she asks, "So you went out with a friend tonight? What'd y'all do?"

It's not exactly the third-degree, but I do sense that Whitney's doing her brother's dirty work, trying to figure out the nature of my relationship with Troy and what we did tonight that was so *strenuous*. Looking back on it, that was a poor choice of word. No wonder she's curious.

"We went rock-climbing."

Her face lights up, and a bit of tension leaves the room. "Fun! I used to do cool stuff like that before... well, it's been awhile. You're making me jealous."

"Me, too," Blake mutters from behind me. I turn to see him standing in the doorway, holding the frame on either side, watching us. Louder, he says, "Find something?"

Whitney pulls a large Kennesaw State t-shirt from the drawer and holds it up. "This good?"

"It's really not necessary..." I start to protest.

"Yeah—that's good. Okay, I'm going to set the table. See you in a minute." He narrows his gaze on Whitney and pauses a long moment, as if he's reluctant to leave the two of us alone.

What's he so afraid of? His behavior actually makes me *want* to pump Whitney for information on his background.

He turns to go, and Whitney points me to the bathroom attached to his bedroom. "You can change in there. Hand your wet things out—just give it all to me. This shirt will be like a dress on you, so you'll be decent. You don't want to sit around in wet clothes all night."

"Well, I won't be here that long—I was really just going to stop in," I explain through the opening in the nearly closed bathroom door. "I'm sorry that I barged in on your fun tonight."

"Don't be silly. I'm thrilled you're here. Besides, I see that idiot all the time. In fact, I was going to take my food to go tonight, anyway. I have an early work meeting tomorrow."

I peel off my wet t-shirt, sport bra, and skort and pull on Blake's t-shirt. It's way too big for me, but it's dry, and it hangs almost to my knees, so it really is like a dress. I step out of the bathroom, and Whitney gives me an approving glance.

"Cute! I'll go toss these in the dryer. See you in there." She nods toward the front of the house to indicate the dining room and disappears.

I take a minute to check myself in the mirror. I shouldn't have worried about anything happening between Blake and me tonight—I look like one of those memes of a miserable cat forced to take a bath, all wet fur and baleful glare.

Pulling my hair out of its ponytail holder, I shake it out and finger-comb it to help dry it a little then concentrate on wiping the mascara smudges from beneath my eyes. Since that's the only makeup I wore for my date with Troy, there's no other damage left to repair.

I step out into the hallway and overhear Whitney informing Blake of her dinner-to-go plans. As I enter the kitchen, he's studying her face. She gives him a significant glance, maybe checking to see if he approves of her impromptu change of plans.

Apparently he does. He gives her a wide grin and a wink. I've only seen them interact for a few minutes, but I can tell they're close. They seem to share an unspoken language. And now that I'm not in the throes of panic and I'm looking closely, it's obvious they're siblings.

Whitney's hair is darker than Blake's and has more of a brownish tone, but she's a redhead, too, and their eyes share the same amazing shade of green, light and striated with gold spokes. Her skin's much paler, though, milky white while his is more ruddy. She must either stay indoors all the time or live in SPF 70. I find myself intensely curious about her.

"Where did you go to college Whitney?"

She turns around. "Oh—I just went to a small community college near where we grew up. My mom—" She stops and seems to think better of what she was going to say. She darts her eyes back at Blake before continuing. "I wanted to stay close to home, so I didn't go away to school. I went for two years there and then I took online design courses. It all worked out. I have all the design clients I can handle."

"That's awesome. So you decorate houses?"

"Actually, I do more public spaces—offices, restaurants, that kind of thing." She's opening and closing cabinets, looking for something, and stops to glance back at Blake with a grin. "Although I've been known to take on a *few* special private clients here and there. *If* they pay in gourmet meals."

He laughs and goes to an upper cabinet, taking out a plastic, lidded container. That must have been what she was looking for. Then he opens a lower cabinet and produces a paper bag, which he unfolds. He crosses to the stove, fills the container with a portion of Chicken Saltimbocca, and places it inside the bag. Rolling the top of it tightly, he says, "Don't want this to spill on your fancy Jaguar interior."

She takes the offered to-go meal, standing on tiptoe to kiss her brother's cheek. "Thank you, sir." Then she turns to me. "Well, I hope I'll be seeing you again real soon, Cinda. It really was great to meet you. Walk me to the door, Blake?"

The two of them disappear down the hall to the foyer, where I hear low whispers then the opening and closing of the front door. Blake comes back into the kitchen and stops. His eyes flick over me as I sit on a barstool at the counter. He's cataloguing my body in his oversized t-shirt, my bare legs, my bare toes resting on the lower rungs of the bar stool. His gaze comes back to my face and he looks a little dazed, like he can't quite believe I'm here. The side of his mouth lifts as he approaches.

Flutters. Yep, there they are. Only now they're multiplied exponentially because we're actually alone together. In his house.

"Hungry?" he asks softly when he reaches me.

"Starving, actually." I am. But not just for dinner.

As I watch him take out plates and serve our food, I take a moment to analyze myself. I must not be *that* terrified of trying the sex thing with him, because I came here tonight, knowing the subject was bound to arise. Whenever and wherever we're together, the subject is front and center. And I semi-willingly put on his t-shirt when I knew his sister would be leaving us alone.

Maybe I'm just tired of fighting it, and I'm ready to get it over with one way or the other. But I also know this—I won't let this *whatever* between us go any further—definitely not into that bedroom down the hall—until I feel like he's being honest with me. I want to know what he's been hiding.

CHAPTER TWELVE
HONESTY

We sit at the small round table in his dining area, and I'm trying to think of how to bring up the topic. That is until I take the first bite. Then I'm not thinking of anything but the ecstasy being experienced by my taste buds.

"Wow. This is amazing. Whitney wasn't kidding—you really can cook."

A gratified smile spreads across his face. "I told you. And you picked the mallard picnic over this," he chides.

"Well, that was a huge mistake." I take another bite.

As I'm chewing, he's the one who actually gets the conversation started. "So—your date tonight—I take it things didn't go too well? I mean—I guess if it had... you probably wouldn't be here with me."

I swallow and consider how to respond. If I want honesty from him, I need to offer honesty first. "I went out with Troy, a guy from one of my classes at school. We're really just friends. Mostly. I mean, he tried to kiss me tonight... but I didn't let him."

He likes that answer. His expression lifts. "Okay. Good to know. At least *that* one's not much competition."

The flutters are going double-time now. It's amazing how open he is about some things, like his interest in me, while being so closed-mouthed about others. I decide to up the honesty ante.

"You keep saying things like that, but truthfully, there really aren't any others. I don't date much."

Blake swallows the bite he was chewing and shakes his head. "That's hard to believe. I would think guys ask you out all the time."

"I *do* get asked out—not all the time. But usually I decide it doesn't make—"

"Sense," he finishes for me. "What's with you and everything having to make sense? Some of the greatest songs in musical history have lyrics that make no sense whatsoever. Abstract art makes no sense, but it can be beautiful. Some of the best things in life don't make sense. Love is one of those things."

"Well, I've never been in love. I thought I might have been for a little while once but…"

I'm not sure I want to go *this* far with the honesty. Can I really tell him about Tyler? It's so humiliating.

He leans in toward me, his expression soft and encouraging. "What happened?"

I sit quietly for a minute, looking at my plate. Then I decide to go for it. I mean, I'm the one who hates lies and evasiveness, so I'm a hypocrite if I don't tell him the truth when he's directly asking me.

"Well, okay. It's really embarrassing. You're going to think I'm so stupid."

"I promise I won't."

"You haven't even heard the story yet, so you can't say that. So anyway—his name was Tyler. He was a senior when I was a freshman—he was in my sister Kenley's class. And, well, *all* the guys liked Kenley, because that's the kind of girl she is—you'll see when you meet her—she's just ridiculously beautiful. But Tyler... he liked *me*. He thought *I* was pretty, paid attention to me, asked me out, took me to prom. He was my... my first, you know?"

I look down at my plate, abashed. I'm pushing my food around my plate instead of eating it. "I probably should have figured it out—I mean it made no sense. Why would a senior want to date a little freshman girl with no curves and no style at all? I didn't even start to fill out until late in my sophomore year." I shrug, the embarrassment severe now. "I don't know—maybe it was because I was so young, and he was so handsome and a football player and all that stuff—I believed him when he said I was special. I *wanted* to be special to *someone*. And then... after we... you know, slept together, I told him I loved him." I rush through the last part and stop there.

Blake studies me, his eyes alive with interest. "What did *he* say?"

I gulp, trying to ease the painful knot that's accumulated in the back of my throat. "He cried."

"Cried?"

I nod. "He said he felt bad because he hadn't been honest with me. He said he was in love with Kenley and had wanted to get her attention, make her jealous. That he'd wanted her for years, and he was sorry he'd taken advantage of me, but that I looked so much like her. He said he hadn't meant for it to go so far, but he'd gotten excited while we were making out and hadn't been thinking straight. He *apologized* for having sex with me." I shudder, then paste on a fake smile. "Not exactly what a girl's hoping to hear after her first time."

Blake's hand comes across the table to grasp mine tightly.

"So—that's it. My sad, pitiful tale. I've been pretty careful since then not to date anyone when I can clearly see they don't make sense for me. And I've definitely avoided anyone who even looks twice at my sister—which ruled out most guys we went to high school with."

Blake nods, his lips rolling in and then out as he stares at our joined hands. "I'm sorry that happened to you. And you're *not* second-best. You're much more beautiful than your sister."

"How would you know? Wait till you meet her," I tease, joking but not really. Really, I'm still a little afraid to see his reaction when he meets her.

He pauses. "Well, no matter *what* she looks like, there's no way in the world she could surpass you. You are literally the most beautiful girl I've ever seen. Everything about you is beautiful—your fingers." He strokes his thumb over them as he speaks. "Your skin." His fingertips run lightly over the inside of my arm, raising chill bumps over my whole body.

"Your eyebrows when they're raised up into your hairline as you look at me like I'm crazy," he continues. "Your lips, your sky-blue eyes, even your toes are beautiful—I noticed the other night at the grocery store when you wore sandals."

I can barely find the oxygen to respond. "Thank you. I... like the way you look, too."

Okay, that was totally an odd way of saying it, but I've never been accused of being smooth with the lines, and besides, my mind is on what I want to ask him. This feels like a now-or-never moment.

I ramp into it with a little intro. "So... I've told you my big bad secret. Wait—there's one more—I have mother-issues. My mom's... kind of a nightmare. Well, I guess it's not quite a secret. If you ever meet her, you'll see what I mean about her, too. She didn't beat me or anything like that, but she's... never proud of me. I'm a big disappointment to her, while Kenley's always been her darling. And she lies compulsively. Okay—it's all out. And now I'd like for you to be honest with me, too. I really like you, obviously, but I feel like there are things you're hiding from me, and I don't think we can... move on until I know more about you."

His grip on my fingers loosens, and he stares at my face.

"You don't have to tell me of course," I add. "But I'm just telling you that honesty's a big deal for me, and I need to have that before I could possibly consider, you know... getting close to someone."

Not breaking eye contact, he nods. He does the little lip roll thing again, then draws in a big chest-expanding breath and lets it out. "Okay."

"Okay," I repeat, waiting.

"I don't ever talk to people about this. The only people who know this stuff about me are the ones back in Sparta, and my sister. I don't like to talk about it because it's... shameful."

"So that's what was going on with Ronnie. There's no need to be ashamed of your past. I just want to know you—really know you—and I don't care *what* you say—unless of course you tell me you have a thing for my sister—then all bets are off." I give a short laugh at my own joke, but he doesn't laugh with me.

He looks down at the tabletop then back at my face. "You know how you said you liked my truck? And you like my place. Well... you wouldn't like the place I grew up. And my family didn't even have a car until Whitney got old enough to work and managed to save enough to buy an old beater."

"So... you were poor, then. I don't care about—"

"Just listen. I don't think you can even imagine the kind of poverty I'm talking about. My mom was a high school dropout—she had Whitney when she was only sixteen. I came along five years later—different dads. We never knew either one of them. We lived in a trailer park—and not a nice one. My mom—she's not dumb, but she was a teen mother with no high school degree. She never held a job that paid more than minimum wage. And then she started drinking—hard—and she couldn't hold a job at all. By the time I was born, she was a full-blown alcoholic, or at least that's what it sounds like from the stories Whitney tells. I *know* she's one now."

I watch in silent fascination as a tide of red rises from Blake's neck to his forehead.

"Whitney's basically taken care of me all my life, started changing my diapers when she was six, for God's sake. Started babysitting other people's kids when she was nine, and later working after-school jobs so she could buy basic stuff we needed. Mom drank our welfare checks. At least we had plenty of cereal, and American cheese, and bread, and peanut butter from the food bank."

I nod, gaining a new understanding of why he enjoys preparing fine food so much now. And why he's so proud of his truck, Hank.

"Everyone knew we were trash. Kids at school used to make fun of me for wearing the same two shirts year-round—I can only imagine how bad it was for Whitney, being a girl. I got pretty good at fighting, got in trouble a lot. And then baseball came along and basically saved my life. I might have ended up like Mom otherwise. Me and Ronnie and the other boys used to play with some really beat-up equipment at this empty field near the trailer park. One day the middle school coach was driving by the field and stopped to watch. He came and started knocking on doors at the trailers the next day, looking for my mom—he basically recruited me. He was a good guy, a kind of father-figure to me. I kept playing—that's how I was able to go away to school—to go to college at all."

"And then you got hurt and lost your scholarship."

"Yeah, but by then I'd had a taste of life away from Sparta. I knew I'd never go back. I got a job near campus and lived frugally and got through it. I couldn't wait to start working so I could live somewhere decent and afford some groceries beyond cold cuts and mac and cheese."

"Why on earth did you go into TV news?" I know from Kenley's experience that most small-market TV reporters make so little they easily qualify for state benefits.

"I know, right?" he laughs. "I should've thought that one through a little better. But seriously, my journalism classes were the ones I enjoyed the most. I thought I'd be good at it."

"And you are." I take his hand, squeezing it. "I hate that you felt like you couldn't tell me this stuff before. Do I come across as a snob to you?"

"No, but it's clear you come from money. And... well in the past I did lose a girl I really liked over it."

"She dumped you because you grew up poor? What a horrible person."

He flinches at that, making me feel the need to explain further.

"I just mean it's not something that was in your control. And you're wrong by the way—I didn't grow up wealthy. We might have *lived* like we were, with a fancy house and cars and country club membership and all that, but it was all an illusion. You know I don't have a car now, right? My parents always leased our cars, and when their financial house of cards fell down a few months ago, we had to turn them all in. My parents share a car now and live like misers, trying to pay off the mountain of debt they accrued buying stuff they couldn't afford. And I'm working my way through school with the help of a couple of grants and my paid internships. I'd be homeless if it weren't for Kenley paying most of our rent."

He huffs a humorless laugh. "I know you *think* you know how it feels, and you're really sweet to try to "out" yourself as *poor*, but… well, I guess you just have to have lived it to really get what I'm talking about."

His words give me a slight chill. They're an awful lot like the things Momma said, trying to excuse her bad behavior because she grew up with very little money and no father. But then again when I think about it, Blake's response to abject childhood poverty is completely different from my mother's. While she turned into a wild spender and even wilder storyteller, he became an ambitious hard-worker. And he just told me the truth, though he's clearly ashamed of it.

I decide *that* kind of risk-taking deserves a reward. Getting up from my chair, I slip around the table and stand in front of Blake. He scoots his chair out, apparently intending to get up, but I put my hand on his chest and push him gently back into his seat.

He draws in a sharp breath. The haunted expression on his face disappears, morphing into a hungry look that has nothing to do with his unfinished dinner. Without taking my eyes from his, I climb onto his lap, straddling it, putting us face-to-face.

"Thank you for your honesty." I lean in close, letting my lips brush his as I whisper, "I know it wasn't easy."

"Mmmm," he nods, responding to the touch of my mouth by leaning forward and trying to kiss me.

I pull back before it becomes a full-on kiss because I have something else to say. "And now," I announce, "it makes sense to be with you."

Blake gives me a smoldering grin. "That's what I've been telling you."

He slides a hand behind my neck while the other scoops my bottom, pulling me more tightly into his lap. His mouth takes mine aggressively, instantly stealing my breath and firing my pulse rate up to frantic full speed. Then his kiss slows and gentles, turning deeper, opening me, searching me.

With every supple stroke, I'm seduced. I melt against him, my muscles warm and anesthetized. My normally overactive brain empties of everything but him and his deliciously hard body, so big and solid under me. I feel relaxed and hyper-aware at the same time, taking in all the details of the experience—the light scruff of his cheeks under my palm, the muscles moving in his jaw, the searing heat of his mouth, the pleasured groan rumbling deep in his chest. And I feel *sexy*. Sensual and empowered.

There's no question my body is all-in, but my mind suddenly remembers something I've forgotten to confess. And it's about to become very important.

I slide my hands down to his shoulders, exerting just enough pressure to pull my mouth away. "Blake." My whisper sounds ragged. "I have to tell you something else."

He uses the hand twisted in my hair to pull me back to him. "Enough confessions for tonight," he mutters, going in for another kiss.

I shake my head, leaning back again. "No. This one I think you should hear."

He lets out a breath of frustration. "Okay. What is it?"

I pause, not quite sure how to say something I've never said aloud and never really planned to say. "I... suck at sex."

He huffs a little laugh. "What?"

"I suck. At sex. I'm terrible."

His brows draw together, and his mouth twists in a bemused expression. "How can you suck at sex? That isn't possible. You're very sexy." His hands slide up and down my waist as if to demonstrate his point. "You're very responsive."

"Trust me. It's never been good. I just thought I should warn you since you've probably been with lots of experienced girls and you're probably expecting—"

He slides his hand from my neck to place a shushing finger over my lips. "Okay, let's stop right there. Is this about something that douche Tyler said?"

"No. It's not just him. There were a couple others in college. I'm just not good at it."

"Well first of all, stop thinking about what I'm expecting, okay? Because I have no expectations other than being *really* excited about the idea of getting to know you that way... and figuring out what you like. In fact, I've been so focused on everything I'd like to do to you, I haven't even thought about what *you* might do in bed. I don't need for you to be experienced or *try* to be anything. That's not what it's about. It's not something you have to pre-plan. I just want to kiss you and hold you, touch you... please you. Is that okay?"

I nod, my entire body on full-flutter.

"And you can respond however it feels natural for you. Don't think about what you should or shouldn't do. Better yet, don't think at all. When I kiss you and feel you against me, I'm not thinking about anything except expressing how I feel about you— maybe you can just focus on what you're feeling."

I nod again.

"Still scared?"

"A little. I've never done it this way. If I really focus on my feelings and let myself go, I don't know what will happen. I may end up ripping your clothes off and licking you all over or something."

The smolder in Blake's eyes roars to new life and he gives a low groan of excitement, pulling my lower half tightly against his again. "I think this is going to work out just fine."

CHAPTER THIRTEEN
SOMETHING TO TELL YOU

My phone rings at six a.m., startling me and Blake both. I have no doubt who it is. I fell asleep without even thinking to text Kenley, and I'm sure she's just arrived at our apartment to find it empty and my bed unslept-in. She must think I'm in a downtown Atlanta dumpster somewhere.

I jump out of bed and grab my purse, digging the phone out. "Hello?" I'm out of breath, my heart still pounding from the shock of being jerked awake from an incredible dream.

Then I glance back at the bed where Blake's propped on one elbow, his long, lean body only partially covered by a sheet. Maybe it wasn't a dream.

"Where on earth are you? I'm nearly in cardiac arrest, you know. Are you okay?" My sister's voice is high and sharp with worry.

"Yes. Yes, I'm fine. I'm sorry. I just… slept over with a friend."

"You slept with Troy?" She sounds flabbergasted.

"No. Not Troy. I'm… at Blake's house. And I'm fine. Everything's fine. You getting ready for church?" I walk out of the room, partially for privacy, partially to avoid Blake's interested gaze. I'm completely naked and not accustomed to being exposed to a man's view in the bright light of morning. I step into the kitchen and open a cabinet, looking for coffee.

Kenley lets out a long breath. "About to. I just... I can hardly believe this. You never get serious about anyone. And you've never *not* come home before."

"Maybe I've never felt like this before," I whisper. A girlish giggle escapes me, shocking me and no doubt my sister as well.

"That does it. I'm meeting this guy. Tonight. No excuses."

A pause. "I don't know."

"What is the matter with you? Is there something wrong with him? Oh God—he's not married is he?"

"No. And he's not forty-five either," I say before she can think to ask it. "Fine. I'll ask if he wants to come over tonight after work. You can meet him and give him the big sister once-over." *I just hope he won't give* her *the once-over. Or a double-take.*

"Good. Do you need me to come pick you up and bring you home?"

"No. He'll give me a ride home on his way to work. At the station. Where I *also* work—oh God, that's going to be awkward, isn't it?" My hand comes to my forehead, and the cabinet door closes with a soft click.

"Fraternizing. My friend Heidi would approve. And I have no room to judge in that department. Okay. I'll see you tonight, then. Love you."

"You too. Bye Kens."

A pair of large warm hands covers my eyes from behind, and a very large, and very aroused male body presses against my backside. "Guess who?" he whispers in my ear.

"Hmm... let me see? Could it be... Frank?" I joke, using my rotund boss's name.

Blake releases me, and I turn around, laughing. He couldn't look any less like Frank if they were different species. In fact, seeing his fit and muscular physique in the light of day, I'm ready to head right back into the bedroom.

Blake mimes a knife to the heart. "You have mortally wounded my ego. Even *this* might not be able to survive such an insult." He nods down at his arousal, which is clearly oblivious to whatever insult may have occurred.

I step toward him, reaching down between us to grasp the hot hardness. I look Blake in the eye. "He's a big boy. I think he can handle it."

Blake presses his forehead to mine, drawing me against his body with a little growl. "*You* are certainly welcome to handle it. Anytime. Did I hear someone say she needed a *ride* this morning?" His breathing is audible and fast.

I giggle, pressing kisses against his warm chest. "Why? Are you offering?"

Blake grabs my hand and heads back to the bedroom, pulling me with him. "Oh, I'll take you anywhere you want to go... as many times as you want to go there."

# # #

I don't suck at sex, by the way. Not according to Blake. After the first time, he insisted the problem *must* have been on the other end of the equation.

"College guys aren't exactly renowned for their sensitivity and skill," he explained. "I mean—the enthusiasm's there for sure, but most of us don't know what the hell we're doing at that age."

After a few more times, I was a believer. And I'm suddenly extremely *glad* Blake is twenty-four and out of school. Another area in which my faulty *logic* tripped me up.

He's driving me home on his way to work—late I might add—when I bring up Kenley's request.

"So, my sister's dying to meet you. And it's only fair now that I've met yours. You up for dinner at my place tonight? I can't promise gourmet cooking, but Kenley and I can manage something edible I think. In fact, she's like you—she likes to cook, so it will probably be pretty good."

Blake takes a long time to answer, which is strange. *Well, the morning traffic's always a nightmare here. He's got to focus, right?* Finally he says, "Tonight? Man, I wish I could, but I can't make it tonight."

"Oh." I know it doesn't mean anything, but his refusal makes me instantly insecure. "Okay."

Though he claimed that I most definitely do *not* suck in bed and in fact am quite talented, I still wonder. Maybe he doesn't actually want to keep going with this after having a chance to sample the goods.

"Hey," he says, and gives me a concerned glance before turning his attention back to the road. "You know I want to come over. And I will meet her. Just let me check my schedule, and we'll plan something, okay?"

And just like that I'm happy again. "Okay."

"Do you have a home number?" he asks.

"Uh, no. Just my cell, why?"

"No reason. I just wanted to make sure I could reach you. So… you said Kenley works at WNN? That must be cool…"

# # #

We do a decent job, I think, of acting normally at work the next day and for the next couple of weeks, in spite of his frequent trips to the engineering dungeon for help with *technical difficulties*.

Outside of work, we spend as much time as possible together, and not *all* of it in bed. We hang out at his place, go out—it doesn't matter. Wherever we are, whatever we're doing, I'm happy. And now that our respective secrets have been revealed, we talk constantly. He seems just as interested in the details of my life and family as I am in his.

I have to admit, in spite of his desire to work at a network someday and what that could mean for us, this thing is making more and more sense to me. For the first time ever, I'm willing to take steps down a road I can't see the end of. I don't have a map for us, no GPS turn-by-turn. But it's getting harder to imagine a future that *doesn't* include him. Which is scary, but it's also exciting. I've never felt this way about anyone. I'm still fighting the fear that I'm getting in too deep and it will all end when someone better comes along for Blake, but I'm battling through it, being brave, taking chances, and yes—even going to romantic movies. And enjoying them.

That true love thing? I'm willing to allow that it *might* exist after all.

The only tangle is that the promised meet-the-sibling get-together never materializes. Whenever Blake says he can make it, Kenley's not available—she has so much going on with work and wedding planning. And whenever it's a good time for her, Blake seems to have plans. It's frustrating. I mean now that I'm finally ready for them to meet, they're the ones who are keeping it from happening.

I've actually seen *his* sister several times. At her suggestion, Whitney and I went to the rock-climbing gym last week, and we met for lunch earlier this week. Tonight, she and Blake came to see my summer-league lacrosse game. Afterward, he suggests having drinks at a pub called Darby's—apparently a favorite haunt of the Atlanta TV news crowd.

At first I'm worried about going out in my uniform, but when we step through the doors, those concerns disappear. The place smells like beer and popcorn. It's dark and loud and crowded, with a huge bar that takes up nearly an entire wall. The ornate wooden structure looks like it was salvaged from a much older building and gives Darby's the personality of a pub straight out of an Irish village. There's a mixed crowd—definitely a dressed-up young professional contingent—but to my relief, there are a lot of dressed-down folks as well. One table is filled with a group of thirty-and-forty-something guys who must have come straight from the softball field.

I relax, and we settle in for drinks and some greasy bar food. When Blake gets up to get a second round for me and Whitney and another Coke for himself, I lean across the table, raising my voice to be heard above the marginally-talented singer belting out a Taylor Swift tune in one corner. Apparently Friday nights are Karaoke nights at Darby's—good to know so I can avoid them in the future.

"So, I've noticed he never really drinks. Is that because of your mom?"

Whitney gives me a round-eyed glance. "He told you about that? Wow. I don't think he's ever told anyone about her." She studies me over the rim of her almost-empty beer mug. "Do you like him, Cinda?"

"Of course."

"No. I mean… do you really like him? Like, care for him? Because, I know my brother pretty well, and—do *not* tell him I said this—I think he's in love with you. I'd hate to see him get hurt because you don't feel the same way. Or at least feel something close for him. It's okay if you don't—you're still really young. It would just be better to let him know earlier rather than later, you know?"

Her words steal my breath, so it takes me a couple minutes to respond. It's not that she's shocked me—I've been feeling him fall, just as I've been falling for him. I've thought several times he was on the verge of telling me something of great import, and *I love you* seems like the only really big revelation we've yet to make to each other. I'm just blown away by her certainty of his feelings for me.

"Actually, I—"

"Here we are, ladies." Blake slides back into the booth beside me, pushing a full beer toward Whitney and placing a glass of white wine in front of me. "My ears are burning. Are you two talking about me?"

My entire body flushes with heat as Whitney looks at me—anticipation clear on her face. Does she really expect me to reveal my heart's deepest feelings right here at the table? With her watching? Not happening.

"No—we were talking about the stellar *music*," I joke.

He nods and laughs at my sarcasm, obviously remembering my disdain of karaoke and buying the cover story.

I *should* tell him the truth about my feelings. It makes sense. I do love him, and he should know. Especially if he loves me, too. But can I summon the courage to do it? Suddenly, I can't finish my drink fast enough.

Whitney takes a few sips of hers, and perhaps reading the situation, makes an announcement. "Well, I'm going to head home. You newsies have better stamina than we interior designers,

I'm afraid." She gives me a quick wink as she slides out of the booth.

"Drive careful," Blake says. "I'll talk to you tomorrow."

"Oh yes. Call me. I want to hear all the *news*," she replies, giving me the go-ahead-and-do-it look before turning to walk away.

"What was that about?" Blake asks, watching her leave and wearing a baffled expression.

"Um, I guess she was making a joke about news people?" I suggest lamely, though I know exactly to what she was referring.

Now that we're alone, any sort of chit-chat or small talk I might have normally been able to come up with has evaporated. My entire brain is consumed with the idea of telling Blake I love him.

I think about just blurting it out, but that seems wrong, too unromantic. *Maybe I should wait until we're making love later and tell him during? Or right after?* I don't know. I've never said it when I actually knew what I was talking about. The weak feeling I had for Tyler didn't even come close to this. This time it's *real*, and I want to do it right, but I don't know how.

I've also gone into a mini-panic wondering what I'll do if he doesn't say it back. He will, won't he? *He loves me, too.* Whitney said he does, and she knows her brother better than anyone does. Besides, I believe it's true. It's there when he looks at me, when he touches me. *I can do this.* Some risks are worth taking.

I turn toward Blake in the booth, so I can see his face straight-on and he can see mine. "I need to tell you something."

At first he freezes. Okay, probably not the best way to start—Kenley says guys usually freak out when they hear the dreaded words, "we need to talk." Then he lets out a breath and says, "I need to tell you something, too. I've been wanting to tell you. I really should have earlier, but I've been afraid of how you would react."

My heart rate ratchets up to match the beat of the pop tune now playing through the bar. *This is it.* A moment I'll remember forever—we're both going to say those three crucial words. Should I let him go first or should I?

Afraid I'll lose my nerve and mildly concerned about his troubled expression, I take the initiative. "Blake—I... I love you."

For a moment, his face clears into a look of blank shock, and then it melts into an expression I can only describe as one-hundred-percent-reciprocal-love.

But he doesn't say it.

What he says is, "Wow. Thank you."

Thank you? *Thank you? Oh godohgodohgod.* He doesn't love me. I'm overwhelmed with the desire to slink beneath our booth and belly-crawl across the sticky pub floor straight to the exit door.

Then he grabs my hand on the tabletop and brings it to his smiling lips. "I love you, too. That wasn't what I was going to tell you tonight, because I wasn't sure if I should say it yet. But I do. I really do love you."

And life is good again. My heart can re-start, my belly can un-freeze. I can go on breathing in and out.

Blake dips his head and gives me the sweetest possible kiss, a kiss that shows me the truth of what he's just said. That he loves me. But...

"What were you *going* to tell me?"

He lifts his head, and that troubled look is back in his eyes. "I don't know if now's the time to talk about it. It never seems to be the right time."

I kiss him gently then draw back, staring into his eyes. "Remember what I said? You can tell me anything. So don't be afraid. Whatever you have to say won't change how I feel about you."

"Well..." A long pause. He takes a deep breath, "I hope that's true because—"

"Cinda?" A new voice enters the conversation—one that millions of Americans know and love—because it belongs to Larson Overstreet, my sister's fiancé.

"Shit," Blake mumbles, his face stricken and draining of all color.

I turn my head to see Larson and Kenley standing beside our table. "Kenley," I exclaim. The timing isn't ideal, but I'm excited. Here, without planning anything, I finally have the chance to introduce her (and her true love) to *my* true love.

But she's not looking at me. Instead, her eyes are locked with Blake's, and she looks absolutely devastated.

"I'm so sorry," she whispers to him.

CHAPTER FOURTEEN
NOW I GET IT

"Kenley?" I stare at her, struck to the core by her horrified expression. Glancing at Larson's face, I see he's as clueless as I am. Then I turn back to Blake. "Blake? What's going on? Why is she telling you she's sorry?"

And then it hits me.

They've met before.

They *know* each other.

Very well.

Reading his eyes as well as the face of the open, transparent girl I've known my entire life, I know what Blake was afraid to tell me. He *is* Kenley's Blake after all.

Even though he claimed to have gone to a different college, even though he never admitted it—*she* was the girl he was so hung up on in school, who dumped him when she found out about his impoverished background. She was the one he was so upset over losing.

My heart liquefies and drains out the soles of my feet. I am second-choice once again. The consolation prize. An also-ran who happened to win the race because the lead horse tripped and broke an ankle. He didn't want *me*—he wanted *her*—and I am the closest available substitute for her perfection.

I scramble out of the booth and charge past Kenley and Larson, ignoring her pleading voice as she calls my name. The bar is even more packed than when we arrived, and I feel like I'm trying to get down the lacrosse field toward the goal with aggressive defense players blocking my way. I finally shove through and reach the exit door, but before I can push it open, a thick arm goes around my waist and stops my forward motion.

Blake's voice is at my ear. "Please. Let me explain."

I lunge forward, breaking free of his restraining hold, and burst through the door out to the sidewalk, where I plan to do—what? I'm not sure. Maybe catch a cab, though I have no wallet since I'm in my uniform.

Blake is right on my heels, joining me out in warm night air that's thick with humidity and tension.

His face is haunted, his pupils so dilated the green of his eyes almost disappears. "Cinda—you've got to let me explain. I'm sorry I didn't tell you sooner. I know I should have."

"Yes. You should have. And then we could have avoided this whole stupid thing." I turn away from him, searching the street for a miracle-cab to appear through eyes blurred by tears. *I can't believe I'm living this again.* It's like being in a real-life version of Edge of Tomorrow or the Star Trek: The Next Generation "Cause and Effect" episode.

Blake's hand comes to rest gently on my shoulder. I jerk away from his grasp, spinning to face him. "You *lied* to me. You know how I feel about honesty. You said you went to school at Kennesaw, but you went to UGA with Kenley."

"I did graduate from Kennesaw. I *had* a baseball scholarship to Georgia, and like I told you, I lost it when I got hurt. So I transferred. But I'm not trying to make excuses. I know leaving facts out is as bad as lying. I just… I knew how you felt about people who've dated your sister… and I liked you so much. I didn't want you to reject me over something that happened in the past before we even got a chance to know each other. I would change it if I could. I wish I'd never met her."

My response is a bitter snarl. "I bet. Because you've never been able to get over her—like everyone else—she was your *dream girl*, and you lost her."

"No. No Cinda. It wasn't like that. I liked her—I thought she was pretty and nice. But there was never anything serious between us. I never felt anything for her even close to what I feel for you. I *never* loved her. But I love you. I love you, Cinda. Please forgive me."

I wipe angry tears from my cheeks. "And I'm supposed to believe this *why*? Because I can trust you so much? Because you've been so honest with me?"

Motion in my peripheral vision catches my eye. I realize Kenley and Larson have followed us out of the bar. When I glance at her, she speaks up, tears running down her face and streaking her mascara to tragically beautiful effect. I can't even cry without being one-upped by her.

"He's telling the truth. There was nothing between us. It never went very far. We only had a couple dates before I met Mark."

Now my ire is directed at her. "You were in on this… cover-up, or whatever it is. You knew who he was from the beginning, and you didn't tell me—even after what happened with Tyler. I can't *believe* you didn't tell me."

"I *didn't* know from the beginning. You never said his last name, and I didn't see him on TV until much later—you know my show is on at the same time as your six p.m. newscast."

"You should have told me as soon as you knew!"

"That's my fault," Blake interjects. "I called her at WNN and begged her not to tell you—to let me tell you first. Believe me—she didn't like it. But when I told her how much I care for you and how important it was, she agreed to wait a little while."

"*That's* why I could never get you two in the same room." All my illusions are popping like helium balloons drifting into the night sky. "You sure did work well together—coordinating your campaign of betrayal. Kenley—you sure about this thing with Larson? You and Blake here make quite a *team*. Maybe you should reconsider your engagement." My voice sounds vicious, almost unrecognizable to my ears.

The poisonous arrow hits pay dirt. Kenley isn't trying to argue on Blake's behalf anymore or even defend herself. She's weeping openly.

Larson pulls her in to his chest, stroking the back of her head and murmuring in her ear. Perfect. She gets to have *both* guys—the one she plans to marry and the one who wishes it was him instead.

And what about me? What do I get? A night in my parents' guest room for starters.

# # #

"Do you really think those sites work?" asks Momma as she studies the laptop screen over my shoulder. I've been home for twenty-four hours, and already she's driving me insane. She's picked on my clothes, my hair, and now my chosen method of dating. Honestly, I could care less about finding someone new to date—the thought turns my stomach—but it's the best way to move on. And I *have* to move on. Moping around thinking of Blake every waking moment isn't doing my sanity any good.

"Lots of people find partners this way." I shrug and click on another picture of yet another smiling face. This one's decent-looking, and he fits my criteria. "And if I want to find a logical person to date, then basing my choice on a standardized collection of data rather than some random meeting at a bar or coffee shop makes perfect sense."

"I guess so. Do they have financial information in there?" she asks. Of course.

I ignore her question and read through the guy's profile then close it with a groan. He likes romantic walks on the beach. Ugh.

The next guy's profile is much more promising. No mushy stuff. Reasonably cute picture. He's a twenty-one-year-old programmer at a video game company and says he lives near the Tech campus, like me. Perfect.

I grit my teeth, take a deep breath, and click the "Let's meet" button. I know he'll do the same thing I've just done before responding—read my profile and check out my picture. I posted one that Kenley took of me on Easter. As usual I'm wearing no makeup, but the lighting's good and my eyes really show up.

At the thought of Kenley, my gut rolls. Partially with disgust but also… I miss her. She's been the steadiest fixture in my life since I was born, and I've never gone more than a day without talking to her. The rift between us feels as deep and wide as the Grand Canyon, and I don't know how we'll ever close it.

She's called repeatedly, both my cell and Momma and Daddy's phone, but I'm not ready to talk to her. She even came by the condo, but Momma's big mouth came in handy for once. She let it slip that my sister was on her way, and I went for a *long* run, making sure not to come back until I saw her car was no longer in the driveway.

As if reading my mind, Momma says, "I sure wish you girls would work things out. I can't remember you ever fighting like this. I don't like to see you giving her the silent treatment."

"Well, I didn't like a *lot* of things you said and did over the years, so now we're even I guess," I snap at her.

She looks like I've slapped her. Kenley and I were both raised to respect our parents and not to talk back. She was always better at it than me, but even so, I've rarely raised my voice to my mother or lashed out at her. I usually stuff my anger down deep and employ humor to deflect her painful comments. Apparently my sense of humor is out of order tonight.

"Is this about something I've done, Cinda? Because I know I made mistakes. I've told you I'm sorry. Kenley says you feel like that boy Blake wanted her more than he wants you—that I made you feel like you weren't as good as her, and it still bothers you."

Before meeting Blake, I would have denied that. Now I can't. But I'm not even going to bother getting into it with Momma. It's *such* old news. Suddenly, I feel very tired. I close the laptop and push away from the table.

"I'm going to shower and then to bed. Tomorrow I have class early, and then I'll start looking for a new apartment."

She follows me down the hall to the guest room. "You're planning to move out of Kenley's place?"

"She'll be moving in with Larson after the wedding anyway. Might as well find myself a new roommate." I put the laptop on the bed and head for the attached bathroom.

"Oh, dear. This really is bad. Cinda—"

Something about her desperate tone makes me turn around instead of continuing into the privacy of the bathroom, though I really don't want to hear whatever she's about to say.

Her face is stricken, her tone soft and genuine. "I never thought of you as second-best, you know. You were just... so different from me... more like your daddy, and *so* stubborn. So strong—you didn't seem like you ever really needed me—or anyone." She shrugs miserably. "I didn't know quite what to do with you."

There's a long pause as we stand just looking at each other. Then she says in a ragged whisper, "I did my best, baby. I'm sorry it wasn't better. I do love you."

Her emotional confession sucks all the fight out of me. I sigh deeply. "I know."

She approaches me tentatively and reaches for me, as if she's afraid I'll knock her away. I don't. Her slender arms wrap around me, and I hug her back, inhaling the sweet, familiar mom-smell I remember from earliest childhood. It wasn't all bad. And compared to what Blake's had to overcome, life with my mom was a picnic.

"I love you, too, Momma," I whisper.

She squeezes me tighter. After a minute she leaves, and I go into the bathroom and close the door, leaning one shoulder against it in exhaustion. I'm tired of being mad at her, of blaming her. Kenley was right—I have to forgive Momma—if not for her sake, then for my *own*. And she does love me, in her own strange, selective way. I know it's true.

And maybe Blake loves me, too. In an I'll-take-what-I-can-get way. But I want to be loved *better* than that. I want, for once in my pathetic life, to be someone's first choice. Is that too much to ask?

I get into the shower and try not to think of him. Without success. Like Kenley, Blake's been calling. Naturally, I've declined his calls and erased his messages without listening to them, as much as it kills me. It would hurt worse to hear his voice right now.

I miss him. And I still love him.

That apparently isn't going to change overnight. But I have to get over it. This is what I get for acting against logic. Pain and heartache and the world's most awkward work environment.

I wish the hot, streaming water could somehow wash away the feelings that are still swarming my heart. *How will I face him tomorrow at the station?*

I have to go in—Frank has started taking Mondays off as part of his phasing-out, as he calls it. So I'll be the only engineer on duty. If I call in sick, he'll have to come in, and that's not fair to Frank. This was part of the deal for me to have a secure, well-paying part-time job.

I check my laptop one more time before bed, studiously avoiding my email inbox. Mr. Semi-Cute Game Designer has responded "yes" to my invitation to meet. Without any real enthusiasm, I message him and set up a dinner date for tomorrow after work at a pizza place near the station. Great. I'm moving on. Very logical of me.

Then I turn out the light, climb under the covers, and have a very long, very illogical ugly cry.

CHAPTER FIFTEEN
BLIND DATE

"Cinda? Wow. You're like... really pretty."

A slight, dark-haired guy (who I swear I've *never* seen a photo of) rises from the bench in front of the pizza restaurant. He takes a step toward me. He's tentative and seems shy, reminding me of a kitten who's suddenly been approached by a stranger. I'm allergic to cats, by the way.

"Um... thank you? I guess you're Jeff."

"Yes. Yes, sorry. I should have introduced myself. I probably don't look much like my picture. Jeff Slattery." He extends a hand. It's small. Really small.

It doesn't matter, idiot. He's a sensible choice. You saw his data. I force myself to return his smile and shake his hand firmly. "Cinda Moran. I know—it's so hard to tell anything from those little photo files. I probably don't look like mine, either."

"No. You do—just *better*. Most people look worse, don't you find?"

"Oh. I don't really know. This is my first date through the site."

"Really? Great. Great. Maybe it'll be your last." He emits an uncomfortable giggle.

I freeze in place. I think he's trying to suggest that maybe we'll click and be forever-*lurve*-soulmates, but he might also be hinting that he's a serial killer and plans to roofie and kidnap me. They *do* screen for that sort of thing on those sites, don't they?

"So yeah." He giggles again. "I'm thrilled to meet you. Shall we go inside?"

"Sure," I say, but I already know I'm not interested. First of all, I'm considering the possibility he's a serial killer—usually not a *good* sign.

Even if he's not homicidally inclined, there should be some initial spark of interest, right? *You wanted logic, not sparks.*

I nod, agreeing with my internal Vulcan, and step through the door Jeff holds open for me—okay, point for Jeff—I've read that polite men make better husbands. As long as they are not also serial killers.

A hostess seats us and takes our drink orders. I order water. In a lidded cup. Which I will take with me if I happen to go to the ladies' room during dinner to prevent the aforementioned roofie-ing.

Jeff orders a bourbon and coke. I estimate he can handle about one of those with his body mass index. Maybe half. I'm sure he's nervous. Maybe he's afraid I'm a serial killer, too. Whose wonderful idea was this again?

On the upside, the deep-dish pizza is delicious. I dive right in, not worrying about what Jeff thinks of my eating habits or whether I have sauce on my chin. There could be *some* value in being with someone whose opinion I don't give a flip about.

On the not-so-upside, things don't get a lot better conversationally. The video game stuff is pretty interesting. For a while. And then it's too technical, even for me. I *am* happy for his gaming customers, though. The guy is passionate about his work. And about his cats. All seven of them.

"So I wake up, and Dipsy is licking the inside of my ear—not the top part, you know, but like deep down in the ear canal—"

"Hold that thought," I interrupt before that deep-dish pizza can make a spontaneous encore appearance. I slide out of the booth, holding up my plastic cup. "I'm going to grab a refill."

As soon as I'm on my feet I see Blake standing in the restaurant's entryway. He's scanning the room, and then our eyes meet. I avoided him all day at work, going so far as to lock the engineering office when I was inside. But now here he is—he must have followed me from the station or something. I look around the room. There's nowhere to go. Well, I do see a sign for the ladies' room, and I might make it there before Blake reaches me if I sprint. But knowing him, he'll just wait me out.

He approaches our table—and I can't help myself—I watch him the whole way. *God, the way he moves.* Just seeing him walk through a pizza parlor makes me flash back to being in bed with him, enjoying that big athletic body—minus the suit. I guess the lust doesn't go away instantaneously, either. Well, I'll have plenty of time to work on it because no matter what he says—

"Cinda—for God's sake—please let me talk to you. I'm dying here. You have *got* to give me a chance," he pleads when he reaches me.

"Excuse me." My date has now gotten out of his side of the booth and is bowing up to Blake's much bigger form. His tiny hands are firmly planted on his hips, making him look like an irate cartoon chipmunk.

Blake gives him a cursory glance then his eyes immediately come back to mine. "Please. I love you. I've never felt this way about *anyone* before—certainly not your sister."

"What's going on here?" my indignant date demands. "Your profile said you were *not* in a relationship."

I speak to Jeff but keep my eyes trained on Blake. "That's true. He's... no one. No one important to me, anyway." The lie makes my stomach clench, but I stand firm, not allowing my gaze to waver.

Looking stricken by my cold-hearted description of him, Blake continues nonetheless. "You can't just walk away from this."

"I can and I did." Now, I turn to Jeff. "I'm not in a relationship. He's my ex."

"Well, then," my blind date clears his throat and straightens to his maximum height, still not quite reaching Blake's, but I have to admire the effort. "I'll have to ask you to leave. We were enjoying a nice dinner date—"

He has finally succeeded in getting Blake's attention. And probably regrets it. Blake turns to him, towering over him with his fists clenched. His voice is low and practically a growl as he addresses his *competition*. "The date's over, friend. I'll pay the tab. Why don't you go on now? She'll call if she's interested."

Jeff glances nervously over at me, clearly intimidated and tempted to accept Blake's dismissal.

I feel bad, but Blake's right—there's no way our date could continue after this, even if I *was* interested in Jeff. I nod to him. "It was nice to meet you, Jeff. Good luck with your games... and Dipsy." Bringing my gaze back to Blake I add, "And *I'll* pay the tab."

I know exactly what happened to the spark that was missing when I met Jeff—Blake took it. He took them all. Every spark I'm capable of feeling has apparently been commandeered by the large angry male in front of me.

"Here or my place?" he demands.

"What?"

"We're going to talk. Here, my place, your place, work… the ladies' room," he adds as he notices my eyes dart in that direction.

I let out an aggravated breath. "Fine. We'll stay here." In public. If we go somewhere alone together like his place (or even the ladies' room), my body will want to forgive him in spite of what my brain says. I can't deny that I want him. It's just a fact. Facts are what they are.

But I will not make any more decisions based on feelings. My recent departure from logic has ended in disaster, and I won't make that mistake again. And I've decided it's logical for me to go ahead and talk to him now, because apparently that's the only way he'll ever leave me alone.

We both take a seat, and I speak before he can start. "You and I don't make sense." I fold my arms in front of me and discipline my face into an emotionless mask.

Blake leans toward me, speaking in a fierce whisper. "We love each other. What doesn't make sense about that?"

I shrug. "With all the men out there in the world who *haven't* dated my sister, it isn't logical for me to choose to love one who *has*."

"Choose," he repeats, his voice dripping with derision. "You don't *choose* who you're going to fall in love with. You love who you love. And you told me Friday night that you love *me*. We belong together, Cinda. If I could go back in time like Kirk did in The City on the Edge of Forever episode, I would—and I'd unmeet Kenley. I'd run when I saw her coming. *You* were the one I was destined to meet. You're the one I was meant for. "

I shake my head, staying strong on the outside, while my insides are screaming *Amen, that's right,* like some country-church gospel choir.

"I don't believe in meant to be. And I don't believe in one person for everyone. It's just science." I nod. "Yes, we have good chemistry, but it's nothing more than that."

He holds my challenging stare, meeting it with a calculating gaze. Then he rises and leans over the table, grabbing the back of my head in one huge hand and pulling my face to his. He crushes my lips with a kiss, and in spite of my best intentions, my lips part and my tongue meets his, hungry for him, participating fully in a clear act of mutiny against my brain. After a minute Blake pulls away and drops back into his seat, wearing a satisfied expression that tells me he believes he's made his point.

I take a couple of slow breaths, then controlling my voice so that it sounds wholly unaffected, I say, "Chemistry. Pheremones. That's all I feel."

Blake shakes his head in an angry gesture. "You really are Miss Spock if you can turn off all your feelings just like that. I thought there was a human being in there, but maybe you're all Vulcan."

As much as I've always enjoyed the comparison to my favorite TV character, at the moment it stings. Of course I have feelings. And this guy stomped all over them by deceiving me. I just stare at him, daring him to get up and go. Why would he stay if he thinks I'm an emotionless void?

Blake breaks first. His whole body slumps then he leans toward me, reaching across the table. "Cinda—please. Give me another chance. I'll never omit another detail about my life. You want to hear about all my mom's shitty boyfriends and how Whitney and I had to push a dresser in front of our bedroom door every night to keep them from getting in to her... to me?"

I keep up my stoic stare, but it's not easy. Not with him baring his soul across the table. I wish he would stop, but if I open my mouth, if I move an inch, I'm going to cry and give in.

"You want to hear about... how I've never wanted to need anyone in my life? Because the person I *did* need—the one I depended on—wasn't there for me? I've got a whole closet of therapy journals. You can read them all. You can ask me anything, and I'll tell you the truth."

He swallows and takes a breath before continuing. His voice is ragged now, and it's ripping little pieces of my heart with its sharp edges. "The biggest truth is that I need *you*. That scares the shit out of me to admit—but it's true. I finally let myself need someone, love someone to the point that you can hurt me worse than my no-good drunk mother ever did."

Oh God. This is terrible. I want to climb over the tabletop and plaster myself to him. But I promised myself *never again*. I do love him. I do need him, too. But I don't *want* to need someone I'm not sure of. Someone with the power to hurt me with a lie the way Blake has already done. The way Momma did my whole life.

I can't know that he won't do it again. When I put logic on one side of the risk scale and my heart on the other... there's no contest. Logic is heavier. I'm tempted to lean on the other side, to cheat and make the scale at least even out... but I decide to go with what I know—with what's always worked for me before.

"I'm sorry," I say. "I can't do it anymore."

Blake sits perfectly still for a moment, staring at me, maybe letting the words sink in. Maybe making sure I mean them. And then he slides out of the booth and walks away, leaving me with half a greasy deep-dish pie and a broken heart.

Thanks, logic. You're a real pal.

CHAPTER SIXTEEN
SALVAGE OPERATION

For the rest of the week there are no knocks at the engineering room door. I stay away from the newsroom as much as possible, and Blake stays away from me. I keep thinking this is going to get easier, but so far it just keeps getting worse.

I may have made a sensible decision, but good sense isn't much comfort when I'm crying myself to sleep every night, missing him, missing my sister, missing having a heart that actually feels things instead of simply clicking mechanically along like some sort of clockwork device.

Even Frank's friendly presence at work and my ever-faithful Enterprise crew are no match for the misery that's overtaking me. I can't even study for my classes—it's hard to care about thermodynamics when my entire future looks like a black hole.

Friday is another one of Frank's phase-out days, so I'm in the engineering department alone when the phone rings.

"Hello."

"Um, Cinda? It's Alissa at the desk. Are you sick? You sound like Hell."

"No. I'm fine. What is it?"

"Well, bite my head off. Okay, well, there's this lady here to consult on the new set design, and she has some questions about lighting placement and, like, electrical stuff. So since Frank's off today, they need you in the studio."

"All right." I groan, reluctant to leave my safe little dungeon. "Tell them I'll be right up."

I trudge upstairs and toward the studio, avoiding the newsroom. When I step into the studio, I don't see the set designer at first—the woman's off in a corner, conversing with two of the carpenters who've been working in here for the past week tearing out our old news set, and their much-larger figures are blocking her face from my view.

Then one of them steps away, and I see... "Whitney?" My voice sounds strangled. "What are you doing here?"

Just looking at Blake's sister is painful, her beautiful face and dark auburn hair a heart-stinging reminder of the only guy I've ever loved.

She comes toward me, all smiles, maybe for the sake of the workers around us. When she reaches me though, she drops the pretense. But she doesn't look angry, doesn't *appear* to hate me. Instead, her face is filled with compassion.

Her voice is soft and low when she speaks, the words meant only for me. Her hands wrap around mine, imparting a hint of warmth to my ice-cold skin. "Cinda. How *are* you?"

Glancing back over her shoulder, she addresses the carpenters. "Hey guys—want to go ahead and call it a day? This consult's gonna take a while. See you Monday morning."

The men get up and leave the room, appearing not to mind leaving early on a Friday at all. Whitney walks over to the carpeted base of the old set, the only part of it that remains. She sits down and pats the surface beside her.

"Come here. Let's chat."

I finally find my voice. "What are you doing here?" I repeat, woodenly obeying her instructions and lowering myself to the riser.

"I'm consulting on the new set design. The news director decided he wasn't an interior designer after all—after being torn a new one by the general manager—or so I hear. Blake suggested that I might be able to help *without* killing the project's budget, so they called me..." She drops her chin and looks directly into my eyes. "I'm here to *try* to help salvage things."

The way she says the last part makes me wonder if she's here to salvage the set project or something else. The look in her eye confirms it for me.

"So... you know what happened, I guess." To my shame, I'm having to battle my tear ducts for control.

She nods, and her eyes are glistening with pity. "You look terrible—sorry—you know what I mean. And I've never seen Blake like this. I've dropped in to check on him every night this week— though he keeps telling me to go away. He's stopped cooking. When he eats at all, it's plain tuna out of the can. He even ate peanut butter crackers the other night."

I look away from her sad eyes. "He'll get over it."

She shakes her head. "I'm worried about him, Cinda. He's saying things like he might move back to Sparta and find some kind of a job there. And last night... he was drinking. Alone. It's like he feels so bad about what he did to you he's given up on himself. I don't know what to do."

And now my heart's ripped totally out and lying on the sawdust-covered studio floor. What he did to me? What about what I did to *him*? I shut him out completely, slammed the door to my heart without really even listening to him.

"I think you should know... he never mentioned your sister to me back when he was in college. You're the only girl he's ever talked to me about. He was desperate for advice on how to win you. He loves you, Cinda. I hope you believe that."

"I'm... too afraid to believe it," I admit.

She shakes her head. "That doesn't sound like the Cinda I've gotten to know. You've told me how you stood up to your mother's pushiness all these years, how you made up your mind to get into Georgia Tech and work your way through school no matter what it took, how you've worked at all these big companies. It takes a very courageous person to do all those things, a person who believes in herself. So why can't you believe Blake could love you?"

I stare at Whitney's gentle expression, processing her words. Blake *told* me he loved me. More importantly—when I look back on our relationship—he's *shown* me he loves me. And he showed me I'm capable of loving someone, too. That it's *real* and not just a decision people make because the numbers add up and the data supports it.

My face drops into my palms and my shoulders sag. I rock back and forth. "What should I do? I've been... horrible. I don't know if he'll even want me anymore."

She gives a little half-laugh, half-sob, rubbing my back. "I wouldn't worry about that. He's never wanted anything so badly in his life—and this is an ambitious man. He definitely wants you back, but I should warn you—"

At her serious tone, I lift my head.

She winces. "He's... um... he's moving through the stages of grief pretty quickly. He's zipped through denial and bargaining right to anger. That one may last a while."

"Oh." I picture Blake's fierce, incredulous expression when I refused to show any emotion at the pizza parlor. I imagine how he might react if I approach him now, after the way I've treated him.

Instead of being intimidated, I feel a growing sense of determination. Whitney's words have galvanized me. And if I've been strong enough to hold up under Momma's scorn all these years, then I can handle some blowback from a guy who's entitled to it.

I sit up straight and face Whitney. "It's okay. It doesn't matter. I don't care what he says—I've got to tell him that I'm sorry for my part in this. And tell him I still love him."

"You do?" Whitney's eyes fill, and she reaches around me and squeezes tightly. "Thank God." She lets go and leans back on her hands, blowing out a long breath. "I've never felt so helpless in my life—well, that's a lie—but not for a long time."

"You're sure he still loves me?"

"As sure as I am about *this* being the first and last time I ever take on a design project for free." She gestures around at the teardown around us. "This project is a mess."

"Oh no. You're not getting paid at all? You came here just to talk to me, didn't you?"

She gives a dismissive wave. "I don't really care about the money. The most valuable thing anyone could give me at this point is my brother's happiness."

I stand up and start toward the newsroom, ready to re-open my heart, ready to feel Blake's arms around me again. "I'll go talk to him right now."

She stands, too. "He's out on a live shot. But I do happen to know where he'll be after work. You remember Darby's, right?"

I nod. "You wouldn't want to come along, would you?" I ask with a hopeful, imploring grin.

"No. I think I'll stick around here for a while. I've always wanted to meet Ian Pence," she says, naming our evening anchor. She raises a speculative brow. "Is he as cute in person as he looks on TV?"

"Cuter."

"Well, then. I may need another *expert opinion* on this set re-design—you know—get the *talent's* point of view." She grins wickedly, looking more like her brother than ever. "This pro-bono job might just pay off after all."

She winks, and I laugh before leaving the studio to go fix my life.

CHAPTER SEVENTEEN
CONFESSIONS

"I'm home." I step through the front door of my apartment—I guess it's still my apartment, though I haven't slept here for a week. I'm hoping Kenley's had time to make it home from work. I really want to talk to her before heading to Darby's—maybe she'll even go with me. I don't deserve her as my wingman, but I sure could use one tonight.

To my relief, she rushes from her room into the living area. "Cinda! Wow. I didn't expect—didn't know—"

Before she can even complete her garbled train of thought I close the distance between us and hug her. She stiffens in surprise for a moment, then her arms come around me and she hugs me back.

"I'm sorry," I say into her hair. "It's not your fault."

She pulls back so she can see my face. "*I'm* sorry. I should have told you right away—as soon as I realized who he was—no matter what he said."

"No. I understand why you didn't... and why he didn't want me to know. He knew I'd react exactly the way I did. For all my attempts at being logical, I've acted like a crazy person over this."

"You're not crazy. You're just in love. It makes us do some crazy things sometimes—believe me, I understand. I didn't realize you were still struggling with the thing over Tyler, though. You've always seemed so strong to me, so secure, like nothing really bothered you."

"Yeah—Miss Spock—that's me. I'm just an expert at denial, I think. But I'm done with that."

"What changed your mind?"

"Blake's sister Whitney came by the station. We talked, and I realized I've hurt him at least as much as he hurt me. And there's no need for it. If he can be brave enough to overcome his momma-issues and move forward, I can overcome mine, too. And there's something else I've realized I need to get over... so I'll go ahead and admit it. I'm jealous of you. Or I *was*."

Her jaw drops. "Jealous? For God's sake *why?* Because of Momma's attention? Believe me, you were better off not being her 'favorite.' I was always envious that you were able to fly under the radar so much better than me."

"No. It's not that. I was jealous because you're always so beautiful and poised and perfect, because every guy we knew wanted you instead of me."

"That's not true. I've never been perfect, and *you*—you *are* beautiful. You don't even need all this gunk I plaster myself with." She uses a hand to gesture toward her made-up face. "As far as guys go... I never told you this, but Mark used to check you out all the time when he thought I wasn't looking. And he was a little *too* disappointed whenever we'd have a family thing and you weren't there. I was super-jealous of you."

"Wow. I didn't think I could hate that guy any more than I already do. I was wrong."

Kenley laughs. "And let me tell you something about *Blake*," she says shaking her head for emphasis. "He was interested in me when we met in school, but the way he feels about you is a whole different thing. He *never* had that much intensity about me. Even if I hadn't met Mark, I doubt Blake and I would have kept going out. And just in case you're wondering—we never… you know."

I giggle, my gaze going up to the ceiling and back down to her. "Okay. That *is* good to know, actually. I mean, I have my limits where hand-me-downs are concerned."

Her face lights up. Her tone is filled with hope. "So does this mean you're going to get back together?"

I take a deep breath and lift my palms in front of me. "I hope so. Whitney said he'll be at Darby's tonight. I'm going there in a few minutes to apologize and to see if he still wants me."

Kenley claps her hands and does a little tippy-toe happy dance. "Of *course* he does. He's not a double-engineering major, but he's no dummy either. Come on. I'll drive."

CHAPTER EIGHTEEN
ELVIS

The sound of a beached and desperate whale is audible before we even open the door to Darby's.

Oh, not a whale. Once inside I can see that it's actually a girl singing—if you can call it that—up on the small stage in the front of the bar. She's super-tan, super-skinny, and wearing a get-up that would make Miley blush. Right. Friday night Karaoke.

Fine, I'll just have to make my heartfelt let's-stay-together speech to the accompaniment of Katy Perry's most recent hit song, minus the actual melody.

First I have to find Blake. Thankfully, it's not hard. Kenley and I take a few steps into the place, and his auburn curls catch my attention. He sits a head taller than the people surrounding him in a long booth against the wall. Blake's back is to me, but I can see the faces of a few of our co-workers from the station.

Luce is one of them, thank goodness. Maybe there will be *one* person in the group who doesn't hate me. Gabe's there—Alissa, too. Of course. The top of her little dark head is nearly lying on Blake's shoulder. Well, I don't really care—friend or foe, co-worker or stranger—they're all welcome to witness my groveling if it'll make things right between Blake and me.

Kenley grabs my hand and gives it a squeeze before dropping it again. "I'll wait at the bar. Go." She encourages me with an excited smile.

I've practiced my speech. I know what I want to say to him. I just hope Whitney and Kenley are right and he'll let me say it.

Nerves tangle in my belly, making it feel like a steaming bowl of ramen noodles as I approach the booth. When I reach it, I put my hand on Blake's shoulder and lean down to be heard over the "music."

"Can I talk to you?"

He turns his head, looking down at my hand until I remove it from his shoulder. And then he goes back to his cross-table conversation with Gabe.

Oh no. He's *not* going to let me say it. I've waited too late. He's too furious.

Well, Whitney warned me, and I vowed not to let his justified bitterness stop me. So I step to the side, into his field of vision, and ask again. "Can we please go somewhere and talk?"

Now he deigns to look at me. All conversation at the table has stopped, so his answer is loud and clear. "We *are* somewhere. What do you want, Cinda?"

The beautiful green eyes I've swooned over are dark and hard-looking. Their disdainful stare erases every word of the eloquent speech I've memorized.

All I've got left is a spontaneous ramble. "I'm sorry I didn't let you explain. And I don't even care about the thing with Kenley anymore. I just... I miss you."

He sits there, blank-faced, unmoving. Unmoved. *It's not working.*

Suddenly I remember the main gist of my prepared speech. "And... I've decided that you *are* the logical choice for me—you

162

were all along, because we're actually perfect for each other. We balance each other out. I realized… if Kirk and Spock didn't have each other, the ship would've gone down in a fiery blaze of space junk, like a hundred times."

The reaction I hoped for doesn't happen. Instead, he stares at me like I'm a total geek—which of course I am—as proven by my Trekkie love sonnet.

Finally, he says something. "That may be true… but I'm not sure anymore that you're the *logical* choice for me. I need to be with someone who's willing to trust me. Someone who loves me."

"But I do trust you. And I *do* love you. That's why I'm here."

"No. You're here because you thought it through and made a decision. You made one of your little pros and cons lists, weighed the options, put us through one of your scientific formulas and decided that the equation makes *sense*. For now. You don't love me because you don't *believe* in love—not the way I do. You can turn it off and on whenever you want to… and I need someone who can't *help* loving me, even when I screw up." He lifts his shoulders and lets them fall, looking sad and defeated. "I want illogical love. I want it all—or I'd rather have nothing. It hurts too much otherwise."

Whitney warned me he was angry. She didn't say his heart had turned to stone. What more can I do? I thought I was demonstrating to him that I *couldn't* just turn it off by coming here tonight, humbling myself, and begging him in front of everyone. And it didn't work.

I stand in front of the table, frozen in place until my co-workers begin to clear their throats and raise their brows. Gabe's blinking in rapid-fire pace, apparently trying not to look at me. Alissa starts to giggle.

Finally, I turn and shuffle off to the bar to find Kenley. Thank God she offered to drive me, because as blank as my brain is right now, I'd never find my way home. All I can think of is *I've lost him. It's really over.* I've lost him.

The dying whale is finally squealing the last painful strains of her song—thank God. All I need to go with my bleeding heart is a raging headache. I'm tempted to cover my ears as I pass the large speaker broadcasting her final note. And then I stop and stare at the stage.

I want illogical love. I need someone who can't help loving me.

Blake's words rush back at me as a desperate plan forms in my mind. I turn in a circle, searching for the sound engineer or whoever's responsible for running the karaoke show. I spot him in a raised booth at the back of the bar and make my way through the crowd toward him. Climbing the small set of stairs up to his booth, I poke my head in.

The guy startles and drops his paperback—a thriller I'd guess from the gun and police tape on the cover.

"Oh—sorry to bother you. I want to… I *need* to sing."

He grins, his close-cropped goatee and mustache making him resemble a cartoon devil character. "Yep. You and every other Arianna Grande wanna-be. There's a list on the outside of the booth. Put your name at the bottom and look through the song catalog. Probably about a forty-minute wait at this point." He reaches for his book again.

I glance up at the stage, where another *chanteuse* is preparing to dazzle the crowd with her vocal stylings. Then my gaze darts to the booth where Blake and friends are sitting. No—*nonono.* He's no longer sitting. He's standing. And it looks like he's saying goodbye to the group.

"No," I practically shout at the master-of-karaoke. "I have to do it *now*. Forty minutes will be too late."

His arched eyebrows lift. "Emergency karaoke, huh?" He chuckles. "What's the big rush? There a talent scout here or something?"

"No. But the guy I love is about to walk out the door—forever—and I have to stop him. This is the only thing I can think of that might work."

His mouth turns down and he nods in an I'm-impressed kind of way. "You're *that* good, huh?"

"No," I tell him honestly. "That bad."

He laughs out loud. "Excellent. Okay, baby. Name your tune."

"Do you have any Elvis?"

CHAPTER NINETEEN
LOVE SONG

Feedback squeals through the club as I grab the microphone from the perturbed singer whose spot I'm stealing and take the stage.

"Sorry," I mutter into the mic.

The opening bars of the old-school song come through my monitor, and I'm squinting through the blinding spotlights, trying to locate Blake. Has he left already? I can't see him, but I have to do this. I have to try.

"Wise men say..." I begin to sing, suddenly mortally ashamed of having dissed the dying whale. That girl sounded like an opera diva compared to the sounds currently being emitted from my vocal chords.

People in the bar, who normally ignore and talk through the singers for the most part, are actually stopping their conversations to listen because it's *that awful*. I don't care. Blake's worth it. If they'd let me (which they won't) I'd come back and do an encore performance every night—I'd withstand catcalls and booing and rotten tomatoes if necessary—if he'd only give me a chance. Give *us* a chance.

Still blinded to most of the club-goers, I continue warbling and wailing my way through the King's beloved hit song, undoubtedly brutalizing its timeless melody. But I put my entire heart into the performance, imparting every bit of love I have for Blake to the words, meaning every one of them right down to the last line... "I can't help falling in love with you."

The music ends, and the place is almost eerily quiet. Did I scare away the entire crowd?

There's a smattering of unenthusiastic pity clapping. But then for some reason, the applause increases and is joined by some *woots* and *all rights*. What is going on? They didn't actually *like* that caterwauling, did they? And then I see why they're clapping.

Blake steps onto the stage, crossing it to join me in the over-bright circle of light. My heart seizes and then starts galloping as he approaches, wearing a look of amusement mixed with... love. I could swear it's love.

He comes close and takes my free hand. "Wow. You really are terrible, aren't you?"

I nod, overcome by emotion and fighting back a flood of public tears that will make my disgrace complete.

"I loved it," he whispers and presses a kiss to my lips. From somewhere far, far away I hear the applause increase. He draws back but leaves his forehead pressed to mine, and his arms clamp me tightly against him. "So... are we having no-fun yet?"

"Yes. And I'd like to keep on having no fun with you... well, as long as you want."

"Well, now. That's gonna be a mighty long time. And *that* means there's just one thing left on the list—unless you think we can find a beauty pageant nearby to stick you in."

I laugh through my emerging tears. "No thanks—I think I've bagged my limit on public humiliation for one lifetime."

"All right then... it's time to meet the mothers."

EPILOGUE

"Guess who?" From behind me, a pair of very warm (and very large) hands covers my eyes, and my favorite voice in the whole world caresses my ear. Blake and I are alone at his place, a place where I've been spending most of my free time lately.

"Hmm..." I say. "Could it be... the love of my life?" I turn around in his arms and wrap mine around his neck, lifting my smiling lips to his.

"Call me crazy, but that sounded almost... romantic."

I kiss him deeply and when he comes up for air, he continues teasing me. "And that felt... well, if I didn't know better Miss Spock, I'd say that felt like... passion."

"One hundred percent illogical human emotion... just call me Captain Kirk from now on."

"I'd rather call you my girlfriend."

"So, it's official then?"

"Yes, it's official. You can put that on your 'pro' list. 'Not Afraid of Commitment.'"

I wrinkle my nose at his teasing and slap his bicep lightly.

He laughs and pulls me hard against him. "Ooh. I'll put that on *my* pro list—"Likes it Rough."

It's hard to stop smiling long enough to kiss him, but I manage somehow. After a few minutes, I draw back so I can take in the complete picture of his gorgeous face. "Blake?"

"Yes, Captain?"

"I hope this doesn't cause a problem, but I have another confession."

"What? You know you can tell me anything," he says.

"Well… I'm sort-of having fun."

He laughs. "Can I tell *you* something?"

"Anything."

He lowers his voice to a conspiratorial whisper. "That was *sort-of* my plan all along."

THE END

AFTERWORD

Thank you for reading STILL BEAUTIFUL. If you enjoyed it, please consider leaving a review where you bought it and on GoodReads Reviews help authors so much!

To learn about upcoming releases from Amy Patrick, sign up for her newsletter. You will only receive notifications when new titles are available and when her books go on sale. You may also occasionally receive teasers, excerpts, and extras from upcoming books. Amy will never share your contact information with others.

Follow Amy on Twitter at @amypatrickauthor, and visit her website at www.amypatrickbooks.com. You can also connect with her on Facebook

The 20 SOMETHING series continues in Book 5, STILL WAITING. Out in early 2015. And you can read Heidi and Aric's story in Book 1 of the series, *CHANNEL 20 SOMETHING*, available now.

Details on the entire 20 SOMETHING series can be found on Amy's website and in her newsletter. In Book 5 of the 20 SOMETHING series, STILL WAITING, you'll experience Jillie and Hale's story as well as attend a wedding! Here's a sneak peek:

STILL WAITING

Since his college sweetheart turned down his proposal, Hale Gentry has been in no hurry to fall in love again. Besides, running his family's large Southern farming operation means he's tied to the land, and anyone who can't deal with that had best hit the road. In his world, your land and family loyalty mean everything.

Now that she's out of college, working and living in her hometown again, rookie meteorologist Jillian Peterson hopes she'll finally have a chance with her lifelong crush. Maybe Hale will stop looking at her as a little girl and finally SEE her. But he seems more dismissive now than ever—finding something to criticize about everything she does, especially her chosen career.

Jillie awakens old feelings in Hale and makes him feel things he's NEVER felt before, not even for his almost-fiancée Heidi. But he's not dumb—he knows what's in the forecast—Jillie's TV career will take her away just like Heidi's did. He's not signing up for a second helping of that kind of pain—if a second broken heart wouldn't kill him, his best friend Beck would.

But when she calls him for help in the middle of the night, Hale can no longer ignore the fact that the girl-next-door is back in town... and more tempting than ever. Even if she is his best friend's little sister.

ACKNOWLEDGMENTS

This is an important part of the book for me, because without the people named here, STILL BEAUTIFUL wouldn't exist.

First, I must thank my husband, who never doubts my abilities and expects the best, and my precious boys, who make me laugh every day, put the joy in my life, and have to be the easiest kids on the planet.

To my lifelong bubba Chelle, who loves me no matter what, to Margie, for being a cheerleader and wonderful friend in every way, and to the Westmoreland Farmgirls, who are always ready to read and celebrate.

I am constantly inspired (and set on the right path) by my amazing critique partner, McCall Hoyle. Love and thanks to the rest of the fabulous GH Dreamweavers and the Dauntless girls for the fun and friendship, and special thanks to my Lucky 13 sisters for their loyalty, good advice, virtual Prosecco, cupcakes, and cabana boys. #teamworddomination. Big hugs and forever love to my Savvy Seven sisters.

Thanks to the talented Gabrielle Prendergast at Cover Your Dreams for another beautiful cover and to Mary and CM for all the good book (and life) talks.

No acknowledgments could be complete without mentioning my first family. I've been blessed to have a mother who made me believe I could, a brilliant and loving dad, a funny and loyal brother, and the best sister anyone's ever had. Thank you to Joanne and Larry, for all the support, encouragement, and boy-clothes shopping! And thank you to the rest of my friends and family for your support and for just making life good.

ABOUT THE AUTHOR

Amy Patrick grew up in Mississippi (with a few years in Texas thrown in for spicy flavor) and has lived in six states, including Rhode Island, where she now lives with her husband and two sons.

Amy has been a professional singer, a DJ, a voiceover artist, and always a storyteller, whether it was directing her younger siblings during hours of "pretend" or inventing characters and dialogue while hot-rollering her hair before middle school every day. For many years she was a writer of true crime, medical anomalies, and mayhem, working as a news anchor and health reporter for six different television stations. Then she retired to make up her own stories. Hers have a lot more kissing.

Amy loves to hear from her readers. Feel free to contact her:

Twitter:
https://twitter.com/AmyPatrickBooks

Facebook:
https://www.facebook.com/AmyPatrickAuthor

Or sign up for her newsletter here at:
http://www.amypatrickbooks.com

The 20 Something Series

CHANNEL 20 SOMETHING
(Book One—Heidi and Aric)
STILL YOURS
(Book Two—Mara and Reid)
STILL ME
(Book Three—Kenley and Larson)
STILL BEAUTIFUL
(Book Four—Cinda and Blake)
STILL WAITING
(Book Five—Hale and Jillie)

Read the back cover blurb of each of my 20 SOMETHING novels by visiting my website, and for latest news on release dates, sign up for my newsletter at: http://www.amypatrickbooks.com/

37487153R00111

Made in the USA
Charleston, SC
07 January 2015